THE WORLD ACCORDING TO PATRICK WHITE

A TALE OF A VERY PERCEPTIVE PIG

First Published in the UK 2023

Copyright © 2023 by Suzanne Stephenson

All rights reserved. No part of this publication may be reproduced or transmitted, in any form or by any means, without permission of the publishers or author. Excepting brief quotes used in reviews.

Any reference to real names and places are purely fictional and are constructs of the author. Any offence the references produce is unintentional and in no way reflects the reality of any locations or people involved.

ISBN: 978-1-915953-32-2

The World According To Patrick White
A Tale Of A Very Perceptive Pig

Written and illustrated by

Suzanne Stephenson

Also by the author

Bearswood End
Mr Perkin's Takes Charge

'Waste' a comic legal novel

Introduction
The World According to Patrick White
A tale of a very perceptive pig

Never let it be said that pigs are not in the public eye. From children's television and stories, to adverts about vegan sausages, there is rarely a day when we don't see something about pigs.

Sir Winston Churchill is reputed to have admired pigs and to have said, 'I am fond of pigs. Dogs look up to us. Cats look down on us. Pigs treat us as equals'.

Various scientific studies have produced results indicating pigs are intelligent creatures, perhaps as intelligent as dogs. The main advocates of the superiority of pig intelligence appear to be animal rights' activists. However, any pig farmer will tell you that any pig is adept at finding where the best food might be and tend to remember the person who brings them their food.

In many cultures and religions pork is unclean. Judaism appears to indicate that in the future pigs and pork will have reason to be accepted. Depending on who you ask, there appears to be some suggestion that Jewish people are not forbidden to have pigs as pets.

There appear to be mixed answers to enquiries as to whether Moslems can keep pigs as pets.

Pigs, like lawyers and litigation, stir up very mixed emotions.

Ambrose Bierce the American journalist from a past age defined a lawsuit as, 'A machine which you go into as a pig and come out of as a sausage'.

But how indeed would a pig view our world if given a full opportunity and what indeed might he or she say?

Chapter 1
Emmie's Diary
First Scribbles

I have decided to start a diary. I live a pretty weird life. I juggle looking after a small farm with being a lawyer. I thought my children might like to read my diary in the future when I get old. They have such busy lives now. We rarely chat and my husband is always involved in some mind bogglingly complex legal case.

Let me explain. I am Emmie Martyns. I am a qualified solicitor and I run a small farm with at any one time between 25 and 50 pigs, about 150-200 hens, 8 geese, a donkey, a pony, and an orchard and a large vegetable garden. I am in my forties (I won't say which end since a lady never reveals her age!). My husband Alain Martyns is of a similar vintage. He is a very successful barrister. He is tipped to become a 'KC' in the near future. I wish I saw more of him. He is always off on some case and his Chambers are in London while 'Babblesprunge' (pronounced Babble Spring) Farm is tucked away in the rural East of England near a little village called Cobblemarkham. Alain has a tiny bed-sit in London which he uses when he is stuck at the Royal Courts of Justice.

Cobblemarkham has a grocery store, a post office, a pub, an antique shop, a village hall, a primary school, a part-time medical centre, a Norman church, a café with an open farm, a tyre and exhaust centre and a population of about two thousand people. The nearest market town is fifteen miles away. The village is pleasant enough but not picture-postcard.

Alain and I have three children, Mathilda, Letitia, and Aaron. Mathilda is aged 22 and studying for the Bar professional exams and she will soon take up a pupillage in Alain's Chambers. Letitia is coming up for the age of 20. I nurture hopes she will become a solicitor like me and perhaps go into business with me. She is studying a double headed degree in Law and Business Studies. Whereas Mathilda is in a horribly overcrowded flat share in northeast London which is part funded by her part-time job in a wine bar and the other part by Alain, Letitia is eking out her student loan in Halls of Residence in a provincial university just fifty miles away. Aaron is only 18 and has just started university this year. He is also doing a double headed degree: Law and Sports Science. He mumbles something about trying to do something in business in the sports world since he is a talented canoeist and sailor. When Alain has time, he enjoys sailing and keeps a small yacht at the local reservoir. I think he inspired Aaron who is now at a rather distant university so he can fulfil his passion for water-based sports.

My dad Miles was a farmer and so I was brought up in the world of farming. Sadly, he is not around anymore. My mother, Rebecca is very much around and breezes in from time to time like a whirlwind. Claiming Jewish-Latvian ancestry Rebecca remains a strong force in my family. She rarely stops more than half an hour at Babblesprunge Farm except when invited for Sunday lunch but will often telephone me late at night and tell me what to do for about an hour or so.

Sometimes she has some good ideas; mostly I just pretend to listen.

When I was young, I worked in a local solicitors' practice, but I had to stop when I had three young children. As they got older, I was able to work part-time but somehow my little farm got bigger and I could not deal with it, a part-time legal job and three awkward youngsters who needed ferrying about. Mum helped when she could in between helping Dad with his farm and being on the Parish Council. Alain's parents were not around to help. Harry and Clothilde Martyns live in France. Clothilde is an elegant, artistic French woman who does not understand my interest in farming. Harry Martyns can claim some French descent, but they live in France to please Clothilde. Harry was a barrister with a significant international practice so until he retired fairly recently, he was used to going back and forth between the UK and other countries. I am not sure how much time Alain spent with his parents as a child, what with Harry travelling and his mother preferring France. I know he spent several years in boarding school. Alain jokes that by means of modern technology he speaks to his father more than he ever did when he was young!

Once our children started to go to university, I went on some legal returners' courses. I felt that I could return to the law, but in my own way. I was aware that there was a dearth of solicitors in my rural area so approximately nine months ago I started my own firm.

"You are mad," said Alain. "Who on earth wants to come to a farm to get legal services?"

I pointed out that many farmers would be happy to come and that I had set up an office with all the usual equipment in an unused sitting room in our house. It had been a playroom and then it became 'the spare sitting room' with some battered old armchairs I had now sent to the tip.

He scowled at me and muttered about no-one wanting a lawyer smelling like a pig. I tried not to be angry.

I had a fairly mixed reaction from the children. Mathilda said on a flying visit, "Oh, Mother, really," and feigned disinterest. Aaron was genuinely uninterested. Letitia, however, said that she was intrigued and wished me well. She gave me a hug and said,

"I would love to be part of it... really... so I hope it works."

Initially I had no clients. Then there was a trickle. I found myself preparing wills and giving advice about grazing agreements and rights of way. It was not going to make me rich, but I had a foothold in the legal profession again.

Meanwhile, my work with the farm continued. I do have a bit of help. 'Scuffy' Dentson comes for about 3 hours each day Monday to Friday and pops in when he can over the weekend. I understand he is really called 'Stephen' but everyone in the village knows him as 'Scuffy'. I asked him about his nickname once, but he just raised his eyebrows and sighed. When he does not work for me, he has a car cleaning and valeting business. I am not sure if his nickname relates to this. His wife Tamzin (better known as Tazzy) spends a couple of mornings a week in my house. When I need a bit more expert help about the animals, we get in Scuffy's dad.

Flemmy Dentson is of indeterminate years, and he retired a few years ago from working as a farm manager. He looks as gnarled as some of the local oak trees. He seems to have an intermittent cough and a quite unpleasant habit of spitting phlegm across the yard. I know his real name is Peter. I have a horrible feeling I know the reason for his nickname.

Some of the animals have names too. There is Mabel the pony and Martha the donkey. The hens don't have names, but number one gander is called Admiral Jellicoe and amongst the geese there are two stand-out characters Tabasco (very peppery temper) and Turmeric (interesting plumage). Did I mention there are house pets too? I have a dog of indeterminate breed who Aaron named Piecrust after my poor hound had rolled in a dung heap when newly arrived and had to have a nasty dried up crust washed off him. The cats are Princess, Duchess and Empress. They are very fine torties and they regard themselves as in charge. Empress is the mother and Princess and Duchess are her daughters who she keeps in check with a firm cuff round the ear.

Then there are the pigs. My two favourite breeding sows are Gina and Lola. They are a good temperament and have been good mothers to litters of little piglets. In early January I acquired my own breeding boar from a nearby farmer Jim Birkshaw. I took Flemmy's advice and bought a fairly expensive boar from him who according to Flemmy was neither too small nor too big. Percival is a feisty brute. Maybe I will have to have his tusks removed. He seems very strong. He has already been mating with any sow or gilt with whom I have allowed him to mate. He has been so enthusiastic I have had to move him away from his lady-friends. He was wanting to hump any female pig on the farm be they a breeding sow or a rather young gilt and was busting down fences to get to them. It was a job and a half to move him. It took Scuffy, Flemmy, Tazzy, Letitia, a rather grumpy Alain, farmer Jim Birkshaw and his labourer Greg, Rebecca, a large bag of potatoes I had grown and myself all of one morning to persuade Percival to go into a trailer so I could drive him all of 200 metres down the track to his new temporary abode. Percival seemed just slightly more amenable when Greg offered him potatoes.

Have I mentioned the layout of the farm? At the front there is a picture-postcard cottage style garden which is a nightmare to weed and a gravel parking area. Then, there is the house. The main building is Victorian. It has five bedrooms upstairs and a nice lounge and dining room downstairs. Someone extended to the side to create the room I use as an office these days, and a garage, and we extended the kitchen at the rear and added a conservatory. There are some brick animal sheds which no doubt were stables built just to the rear of my office. A driveway goes down the side of the house past the brick sheds and joins into the track into our land. We have a large bathroom upstairs with an old-fashioned iron cistern and a modern shower room downstairs plus a septic tank at the bottom of the garden which now and again makes strange bubbling noises. The internet connection is terribly slow. The gutters leak and something always needs mending.

Mabel and Martha have their own wooden stables in their paddock down the track. The brick animal sheds next to the house are used to give the hens some winter quarters but half of it had been reserved in case I had a poorly animal. It is in this area that Percival is now confined, and it has become his temporary piggy prison. I hoped he could have a calmer life away from the odour of 'lady-pig' until I needed his services again. It was a reasonably roomy prison. There was plenty of straw for him to bed down in and a big old stone water trough filled with clean water. Natural light came through the top half of a stable door and using a caravan type solar panel on the roof with battery Scuffy had rigged up some lights for the evenings and dull days.

I would stop and chat to Percival when I could, but being a bit of a soft touch I thought he might get lonely or bored and so two or three weeks ago I rigged up a radio which I left playing to keep him company. I tended to leave it on a news and current affairs station in the day-time and change to a classical music station at night, which I turned down low so we couldn't hear it in the house. Alain told me I was totally deluded. And talking about Alain I need to pause this diary since he is calling me to say "Goodbye" before he leaves on a case.

Alain/work

So, Alain has packed his bag to go to London. He looked genuinely regretful that he was going. However, I know he loves the cut and thrust of the courtroom battle, and it provides a hefty income. My little farm business of eggs from the gate and boxes of joints and chops and sausages for the freezer which I run with the assistance of a local butcher barely covers costs. The excess fruit from the orchard and the excess potatoes and veg which I grow tend to supplement the pigs' diet. I make jams and chutneys and freeze what I can. I tried selling fruit as well as eggs from the farm-gate, but the locals didn't seem very interested.

My legal practice is so new it has not covered its overheads yet, but I have prepared a spreadsheet and if work continues at the current rate, it will cover its overheads within 6 to 9 months. If the work increases, I should make a small income. Alain hopes I will get a part-time role in the local market town but if I can produce a small income, I think he may stop doubting my solicitor's practice. I may have less disapproving looks from Clothilde on our video-calls. Mind you, she has never really liked anything I have done.

Jim Birkshaw wants my help to deal with two things so I shall be seeing him soon. He wants a new will. He has been receiving threatening messages from animal rights' protestors about his commercial pig farm. The police have apparently not responded except to give him a crime number. He has made a complaint, but no-one seems to be looking into his complaint either. Despite the fact he has some 5-600 pigs his pigs seem to me well and content in their surroundings. He has about 3-400 outdoor pigs kept in paddocks up a slight slope away from the road behind his farm. Then he has a huge barn nearer to the road just behind a beet field. The farrowing sows in there have plenty of room to move about with their piglets. But he needs my legal skills to write letters about the failure to investigate his complaint and also a pre action letter to this particular animal rights' group warning of injunctive action if they trespass on his land.

I also need to see Mavis Cuddlestone from the village. She has a problem with a neighbour who has trees which overhang in her garden taking all the light away. The complicating factor may be a tree conservation order.

Letitia says she will come home on Friday so I may have the weekend with both Alain and Letitia. I know Mathilda will be working and Aaron... well he never gives any warning if he is coming. Rebecca may join us for Sunday lunch. If she comes, she may well bring her Red Setter Selwyn with her. If Selwyn comes Piecrust will initially growl and bare his teeth. Selwyn will snarl back. Rebecca will tell me how to look after my dog. Then the dogs will run around the garden riotously having fun and settle down together as best of friends. If Alain is home, he will roll his eyes comically when Rebecca lectures me.

He has only just left, and I miss him already.

Did I mention that it is 31st March? Not long until summer when hopefully Alain might take some time off. Alain often plays practical jokes on me during April Fools' Day. Last year he hid a clock in my pan cupboard before he left on a case. It had an alarm which made cuckoo clock noises instead of a bell. He set it for 7.30 am knowing I would be in the kitchen at that hour. There was a terrible racket from the pan cupboard, I nearly jumped out of my skin and Piecrust started barking loudly. Anyway, I soon found the source of the noise. He had taped a note to the clock which read 'Ha ha, love you and miss you. Look in the laundry box'. I did as I was bidden and found a nice bottle of wine.

I don't know if he will have time to have done anything this year.

Weird, so weird.

I went to bed early. Piecrust slept across my feet. My alarm went at quarter to seven. I began to stir. I went to the bathroom briefly and came back and sat down. I switched on the radio. The announcer said,

"Good morning on this bright and breezy April Fools' Day. First the weather and then the news headlines…"

The weather forecast was good. I turned off the radio before the news. I didn't want to hear a load of gloom. I had a very quick bath while Piecrust looked on. I dried off pulled on my clothes and went downstairs. Empress, Princess and Duchess all lined up by their bowls awaiting their breakfast.

"Miaow," they said in a chorus.

I had a large mug of coffee and some toast and honey while Piecrust munched on some dog biscuits.

It was time to start seeing to the farm animals. Scuffy would be along shortly to help but feeding Percival was my duty. There seemed to be no April fools' jokes from Alain. He had just left a fine Chablis in the fridge with a little note stuck on it 'To enjoy together when I am home'.

I pulled on my boots and slung on an old jacket. I headed outside to the brick stables at the side of the house. The music from the radio was playing softly in the background. A deep melodious voice I did not recognise said,

"Hello."

I looked around. I couldn't see anyone about. I could only see Percival looking at me. Was this one of Alain's jokes?

"Who's there?" I said looking around but not seeing anyone.

"It's me," came the answer. "I'm standing right in front of you, can't you see?" came the reply.

Chapter 2
Patrick's Diary
My beginnings

*M*y person called Emmie has a diary. But I want to tell my story. They tell me I am a Large White pig, not an unusual breed. Lots of farmers keep us. I now understand it's because we grow well, and we are quite tasty. But I didn't know that when I was a piglet. I didn't know I had a name or why I was or where I was. There was just Mum and my nine brothers and sisters.

Mum was big and plump and warm, and we all jostled together for her teats. Sometimes we snuggled on top of each other to sleep. When we got a little bigger, we would chase about and play a sort of tag with each other here in our pen in the barn. I understand from what I learned later that we were weaned at about eight weeks old. All I can remember is that the man who fed us (Tony) came one day with another man (Greg) and picked each of us up very abruptly and put us in a trailer, boys in one half and girls in the other half. We didn't know it was a trailer. It was just a metal box and I remember wriggling and fighting to get free when I was picked up. I also squealed very loudly. I squealed very loudly when I got my first ear tag as well.

For a few weeks I spent time in a paddock with a pig ark with my brothers. I was aware my sisters were in a different paddock. There was stuff called 'electric fencing' to keep us well apart. It was not good to touch it. We were fed some stuff the men referred to as 'pig nuts'. It filled us up but if we could find other things rooting around in our paddock it made it more interesting. Sometimes there were roots or bits of grass. Occasionally the farmer who was called Jim would put in some beets. We even tried earth worm. We weren't fussy. One of my brothers had a bad accident. He was the one the men called 'the runt'. He was rather on the small side and did not seem to grow as fast as the rest of us. He got his head caught in a gap between the fence and the gate and died. I think it was of fright. I think he only got his head there because he was smaller than the rest of us. We would have started to try and eat him if he had not been just a bit on the big side for us youngsters to eat.

I liked Greg. He always spoke to me when he fed us. He seemed to do this if Tony could not come. The men would sometimes talk amongst themselves about 'going on holiday' which I understood was to go to a different place. Even then I wondered what human houses were like. I assumed they had arks like us pigs but more comfortable. Little did I know! As for going on holiday I didn't understand what 'going on a plane' meant or 'getting rat arsed' but 'lying on a beach and having a swim' sounded rather like lying in the sun and having a good wallow.

"Hey, pig," Greg would say. "Reckon you're going to be a big lad."
Sometimes he would give me an extra scoop.

After a while we all grew somewhat. Tony and Greg seemed to be having a good look at us and were talking about us.

"Most of them will be good bacon pigs," said Tony and then he pointed to me. "But that one has big balls and seems a very well-proportioned pig." I swelled with pride even though I did not know what a 'bacon pig' was.

Greg nodded in agreement with Tony. "He might be of use as a breeding boar. If he isn't needed around here, he could either be sold on or slaughtered for sausages later."

I didn't like the sound of this word 'slaughtered'.

"We will have to decide whether to leave him with his tusks eventually. Might be worth getting him checked out by the vet to see what he thinks of using him for breeding. I'll ask him when we next need to call him out," continued Tony.

My brothers and myself continued to grow. When it got a bit colder some extra straw was put in our pig ark. One day Jim came with Greg and Tony and a man I had not seen before. He had some smart overalls and a bag.

"See what you mean," said the man in smart overalls looking at me. "He is one of your better looking pigs."

"Try and separate him so the vet can take a look," said Jim to Tony and Greg. There were some things called hurdles near our field entrance.

Greg called me, "Percival, come 'ere, lad."

"Percival?" laughed Jim. "You might have used more imagination."

I thought so too but I didn't really know much about names then. I knew Greg gave me food, so I came to the hurdled area. All of a sudden things clanged behind me and around me. I started squealing.

"Best be quick, veterinary," said Jim.

I felt myself being squeezed and pressed in all sorts of strange places. I pressed and struggled against the hurdles. Greg tried to offer me a scoop of food, but I was really angry with this vet person. It was all so undignified. I tried to bite him, but Tony had shoved a board in the way.

"He seems a fine pig," said the vet person which made me pleased. Then he spoiled it by saying, "Best let him go before he gets any more distressed."

Distressed? I was not distressed. I was angry. How would this vet person like to be squeezed and examined where he had been looking. I made as loud a grunt as I could but fortunately for him Tony and Jim pulled the hurdles back at that moment and Greg threw a scoop of food into the trough. Food won this time.

One day not long after this Greg, Tony and Jim came with a trailer to the paddock. Earlier in the morning I had heard squealing from some neighbouring paddocks and had seen the trailer going back and forth.

"Right then," said Jim to Greg and Tony, "all of them except your mate Percival."

My brothers were rounded up using pig boards and hurdles. I tried to move forward as well. Greg pushed me back.

"Not you. You're spared the lorry for the bacon factory, today."

Little did I know how lucky I was. Now I understand more I am very pleased my fate was different to my brothers. However, I don't miss them. They were just competition for food. They have served a useful purpose for the humans, and since they did not know their fate, I believe their short lives were happy ones.

I was alone now in my paddock. It was quite nice.

Jim said to Tony and Greg, "Put him to some gilts next week when he has had a chance to settle."

Well, I am obviously not going to go into detail of what happened the following week but suffice it to say I did my duty and kept doing my duty for a while. To my disappointment this activity appeared to stop. It was rather cold weather so that if I had not wanted to bed down out of the cold, I might have expressed my frustration. A few days later Jim arrived as Greg and Tony were feeding the other pigs and myself.

"I've decided to sell that one to Emmie the lawyer. She keeps a few pigs and I need her for some legal work, so I want to keep her sweet," he said.

"I shall miss the bugger," said Greg. "He's quite a character."

I didn't really understand anything other than they were getting rid of me. When the trailer appeared, I assumed I was going to the sausage factory. I charged at people and squealed and tried to bite them. I frothed at the mouth and was as uncooperative as I could be. Nonetheless, somehow, they overcame me, and I found myself shoved in the trailer. As he slammed the door shut, I heard Greg shout,

"Percival, you really are a lucky sod. You are off to see some ladies again and you get a lady farmer too... and as it's a small place you will probably get special attention."

Lady farmer? I had never seen a female human. Maybe things would be alright. As the trailer left the farm and bumped along the road, I could see glimpses of the outside world through slits in the side of the trailer. I could make out large structures which I took to be human pig arks. I have since found out that many humans live in considerable luxury in houses although in some parts of the world they only have rudimentary shelters or fight with each other in things called wars and destroy each other's houses.

The journey was not very long. The last few minutes were even bumpier as we went up a track before I was let out into a small paddock surrounded by fencing which I could see had that painful stuff called 'electric fencing'. It did have a comfy looking pig ark, a big trough of water and a thing the humans called a Mexican hat feeder with some pig nuts in it. Also, I could smell lady pig. The female human and two other men were there. The female was dressed a bit like the men, but she was a different shape and seemed to be in charge. She said,

"Right, lads, we'll give him a few days to settle down before we introduce him to the gilts."

"Thank you, Emmie," said Greg. "Tony and I best be going now. Goodbye, Percival."

It did not take me long to become accustomed to my new abode. A man called 'Scuffy' would feed me. Sometimes another called 'Flemmy' would come. The person I liked best was Emmie. She would talk to me like Greg used to chat to me. It was not long before I had access to the females. Life was pretty good. I was in a nice paddock, there was a nice human who lived just up the track in a big structure I could just see. I had plenty to eat and had girls to entertain me. But after a while that changed again.

I heard Emmie and Scuffy talking.

"He's humped everything he can for now," said Scuffy.

"Yes," said Emmie. "The rest are too young or in pig. We will have to move him to the brick animal shed next to the house. I hope he will calm down with the smell of female at a distance. I would really like to keep him if I can since he is a fine-looking pig. I would prefer not to have to sell him on..."

Sell me on? Move me? I wasn't having any of this so once again I was as awkward as possible. Emmie even had to get Jim and Greg to help her with me. Greg did offer me some potatoes so for his sake I reluctantly gave in and found myself in a brick building next to Emmie's house.

It was quite snug and sheltered and the space was more than adequate although I did wonder why I could not share Emmie's house with her and her family. I had food and I had water and I had light. Emmie would come and chat to me. I met her mate Alain (she used the word 'husband'). He seemed rather wary of me. I met one of her offspring, a female called Letitia who looked all grown-up to me, even though she was spending time with her parents. I understood that Emmie and Alain had two other offspring who sometimes came back to them as well. Human families seem quite odd. It is much simpler in the pig world.

I did a lot of sleeping and eating. I did wish I had more variety in my food than just pig nuts. I gathered there were no spare vegetables at the moment from Emmie's veg patch and it seemed I was not allowed human food. I could sometimes smell human food if she left her house door open.

After a bit I think Emmie guessed I was getting bored, so she put something in my abode which she referred to as a 'radio'. Female humans are not at all like gilts and sows who just have piglets.

The radio sat on a shelf and sounds came out of it. At that time, I really did not understand the device at all. In the daytime it was mostly humans talking and played a lot of what humans called 'the news'. It also played 'the weather forecast' but that seemed a waste of time. A human would tell other humans what the weather was going to do but what they said was usually wrong. 'The news' was mainly about people in charge and also people fighting wars. There were other things too where people spoke, some where one human asked questions to another human. That was called 'an interview'. Sometimes there were what they called a 'sports broadcast' which was terribly dull. Mostly it seemed to be about humans running around after balls, either kicking them or hitting them. There was sometimes a 'quiz' or 'panel game'. These were supposed to be funny, but I don't think I understood human humour; to a great extent I still do not understand human humour.

At night-time Emmie did something to the radio and it mainly played music which I found very restful. She said to me,

"This is classical music... just wait until you hear rock and pop!"

I did not know what she meant then. More recently I have discovered different genres of music. I find myself amazed by the ability of humans to make wonderful sounds and also discordant noises. I would say that given a preference I prefer the works of Beethoven, Elgar and Sibelius. I understand these people are called composers and they make up the music which other people play on devices called musical instruments. Lots of people together playing these instruments is called an orchestra. I wished an orchestra could come and visit me.

However, I did not care for hard rock or "Prog" rock. In my view certain performers of hard rock deserve to be bitten, as did some of the more boring people who spoke on the radio. But I digress.

More recently I have discovered Soul Music. I really like the works of James Brown. It makes me want to jump about and squeal! I would not mind having a go at something like this myself.

The daily presence of human speech was particularly significant. One day there was an interview of a Cambridge professor (a very clever human) about the ability of animals to speak. The clever human was going on about something called the 'source filter theory'. It seemed the production of sounds by animals was a two-stage theory with a lot of variables. It did get me thinking. I now had a much better understanding of human speech. It would be good if I could speak myself so I could make my views known. Emmie is clever but even she has her limitations. So, I tried practicing different noises. At first all I managed was odd sounding grunts and squeals. It took a great deal of effort. I had to really concentrate.

I made sure I practiced this 'talking' when no-one was around. For some sounds I adjusted my grunt. But other noises were produced from my squeals being re-formulated. It was quite tiring and clearly my 'larynx' as humans call it was not used to speech. One morning I reckoned I was ready to talk to Emmie. I did hope she would be pleased when I spoke to her.

"Hello," I said.

Chapter 3
Emmie's Diary
I think I'm going mad.

I stood next to the brick animal house peering over the door which was in essence a stable door. The bottom half was closed, and the top was open. The voice continued to say "Hello" and I could see no-one around. The pig's mouth was moving and there seemed to be grunts between the 'hellos'. I thought that as it was April Fools' Day Alain might have rigged up something with the help of someone else. I opened the door and let myself inside, closing it behind me. I was checking around for wires, cables, loudspeakers... anything to explain what was happening. I found nothing.

"I must be asleep and dreaming," I said aloud to myself.

"Well you look... *snort*... awake to me," said the pig, who snorted again. "I have practiced very hard to talk. It's very difficult."

"Do you think it's easy for me, finding my pig talks?" I found myself replying.

I sat down on a rectangular bale of straw. I was trying to work out what to do. Did I need a vet for the pig? Or a psychiatrist for myself? I was shaking a bit. The pig came up to me and looked me in the eyes.

"Don't be sad... *snort*... I thought you would be pleased," he said.

"Why should I be pleased?" I said still shaking and wondering why I was talking to a huge pig.

"Because... *snort*... I think you are... what is the word? Clever. And your mate and your grown up piglets are away a lot... *snort*... We can be I think the word is 'friends'."

I found myself responding, "I suppose so far as I can be... I can be a friend, but humans don't usually regard pigs as friends even though they are sometimes kept as pets. We are more used to befriending dogs and cats."

"I am much brighter than that stupid dog of yours," said the pig before snorting again.

I could hear Piecrust whimpering just outside the stable door.

I replied, "I suppose you must be to talk to me, Percival." I still wondered when I would wake up.

"I don't wish to be called Percival," was the response. "I have decided I much prefer to be called Patrick. Pigs are often referred to as Percival or Percy from what I hear on that radio thing but not Patrick. I heard that name and I liked it."

"Alright, Patrick. That will be your name," I said.

"I think I should have a second name, like humans," said Patrick. "What breed am I?"

"You are a Large White," I said.

"Pity," snorted Patrick. "It would have been good to have been called Patrick Landrace or Patrick Tamworth... I suppose I shall have to settle... *oink snort oink*... for either Large or White. Which is better?"

"I think 'White' is better," I found myself responding.

"I am Patrick White," said the pig. He snorted and drank some water.

"I have a lot of questions," he said. "It is tiring and difficult talking so I'll start with an important one and after you have answered me, I'll take a nap. Why can't I have human food?"

"Well," I said, "there are laws about what I can feed you. In particular I can't give you anything which might have been in touch with a meat product and that means nothing out of my kitchen."

There was a grunting and snorting. "What are laws?" asked Patrick.

"Rules," I replied. "Rules which if I broke them would get me into big trouble. It might be the end for you too…"

He grunted. I continued.

"I can feed you things which I grow out of my veg garden as long as they don't go in my kitchen and also excess veg from neighbouring farmers that they might sell for animal food. As soon as there is more stuff in the garden I can supplement your diet."

There was more grunting. "I'm having a nap now," said Patrick and he settled down.

I let myself out of his quarters. Piecrust and I got on with checking on the other farm animals. No-one else spoke. Soon Scuffy turned up and helped me with the animal food.

"Noticed anything unusual about my breeding boar?" I asked him.

"Not particularly... He's as crafty as ever, that Percival," replied Scuffy.

"He's called Patrick, Patrick White," I blurted out.

"Who chose Patrick instead of Percival?" asked Scuffy.

"He did," I replied and got an odd look, so I added, "White is for Large White."

The rest of the morning continued in a normal way. After I finished the outside tasks, I glanced at Patrick, and he was asleep. I topped up his feeding trough while he snored. I headed into the house only to receive a call from Jim Birkshaw. He had terrible trouble at his place last night. Despite the warning letters some animal rights' protestors had broken into his farm. It all seemed a bit of a disaster.

Recently he had dug a deep ditch by his beet field to stop trespassers be it the animal rights' activists or people such as hare coursers. It appeared that one of the activists had attempted to drive into the farm via the beet field. His small car had met the ditch and it had ended up stuck there in a near wrecked condition with its front down in the ditch and its back end up in the air. The driver had broken his arm. Nonetheless, his two companions had continued on foot. They had broken into the farm barn occupied by the sows and piglets and sows about to farrow. It seems they wanted to 'free' some piglets. The sows did not take kindly to this. Both men ended up getting bitten, one of them quite severely. Sadly, because of the commotion a sow also took fright and aborted her piglets. Three piglets received minor injuries in the turmoil. Jim, Greg and Tony were quickly on hand and in effect had to rescue the three protestors. The police and ambulance turned up a while later.

Jim was concerned that not only had the warning letters had little effect, but the police seemed to him not very interested.

"I'm sure if I'd got my shotgun out and waved it at the blighters who broke in, they would have had me on some charge. They told me the protestors wanted to sue me for compensation for their injuries."

"That's ridiculous," I responded. "Do you want to come and discuss applying for an injunction?"

"I'll think about it," said Jim. I didn't tell him about Patrick. The rest of the day was relatively normal.

Later.

Rather late in the evening I popped outside to Patrick's shed to switch the radio from talk radio to classical music. As I crept out of the shed a voice said,

"Good night. *Snort, snort...* Emmie."

The Weirdness Continues.

In the morning Scuffy came quite early. We both went in to feed Patrick.

"You're looking a bit pale, Em," said Scuffy. "Is everything okay?" he asked.

"Are you OK?" came a voice punctuated with snorts.

Scuffy dropped his bucket and went a very funny colour.

"Did that pig just speak?" he asked.

"Yes, I did," said Patrick at the same as I said, "Yes he did."

"I think I need to sit down," said Scuffy. He sat down, and a brief conversation ensued between Patrick and Scuffy, with Patrick telling Scuffy he liked him and that he did not wish to bite him.

"I think I better tell my dad," said Scuffy, before phoning Flemmy.

"Hey, Dad," he said, "can you come to Em's place right away? That pig can talk."

Flemmy rolled up about twenty minutes later. He went in to see Patrick with Scuffy and I.

He started to clear his throat and was about to spit when a voice said, "Not in my shed... *snort...*"

Flemmy didn't look surprised, just a bit annoyed. He gobbed into a grubby handkerchief from his pocket and said,

"Here... pig... juss cos' you can talk it don't mean you can always tell me what to do."

"I see," said Patrick.

"You don't seem surprised," said Emmie.

"Sooner or later it was bound to happen," said Flemmy. "What with modern science and that."

"Nothing... *snort...* to do with science, old boy," said Patrick. "I did this all by myself."

For the next couple of days everything just carried on in a normal fashion. My mother Rebecca and I met for coffee at a local café, thankfully, so the job of explaining Patrick to her was delayed. I wondered how I would explain things to Alain when he came home on Friday. When he had unpacked his things, I led him out to Patrick's shed with Alain protesting that he did not know what could be so important.

"I am important... *snort...*" said Patrick.

"Very clever…" said Alain. "Where is the device hidden?"

"I can assure you... *grunt snort grunt...* no device," said Patrick.

Alain looked uncomfortable. "Ventriloquism?" he queried.

"No," I said. "It seems Patrick can talk."

"Patrick?" queried Alain. "I thought he was called Percival? And pigs can't talk."

"My name is Patrick White, and I can talk. How do you do...?" said Patrick.

"For goodness' sake," said Alain. "Always supposing this is not a trick, what on earth do we do? What impression will it give of us if people find out? The lawyers with a talking pig."

"Please stop being cross," I said. "Maybe we can learn from this."

Alain raised his eyebrows. Patrick looked straight into Alain's face.

"Don't be, *snort,* cross with Emmie, she is very kind. I don't want to have to bite you."

Alain looked Patrick back in the eye. "If indeed this is not a trick if you ever bite me or Emmie or any of my family you will definitely become sausages."

I intervened. "Patrick, I want you to respect Alain. It is very important to me."

There was some grunting. Then Patrick said, "Sorry."

Alain just raised his eyebrows and then he started making for our house saying, "I think I need a strong drink." I could not help thinking I needed a strong drink too.

I spent the evening persuading Alain that we were not mad and that it was fascinating and unique to have a talking pig. Letitia was due to turn up very late and by the time she arrived and after a nice Rioja, a steak and a Scotch, Alain had mellowed.

I very slowly explained to Letitia what had happened.

"You are not joking are you?" she said. I confirmed I was telling the truth. She seemed very calm.

"Do you want to come with me and see if Patrick is awake? I leave a radio in the shed. It has news and chat in the day, but I switch it to music at night," I said.

She followed me into Patrick's quarters. He looked rather sleepy.

"Hello," said my daughter, "I'm Letitia."

"*Snort grunt* hello, how nice to meet you," said a sleepy pig.

"Nice to meet you too. Is it good or bad to be able to speak with humans?" probed Letitia.

"It's very mixed," said Patrick. "I find the human world very confusing. I don't think other pigs can talk like me and that makes me think I am all on my own. *Grunt.*"

"Oh poor you, how sad," said Letitia who to my dismay went right up to Patrick, bent over him, put her arms around him and gave him a big hug. Despite his ability to speak, Patrick was after all a massive great boar with tusks.

However Patrick gave a helpful response. "I am rather tired now," he said. "Come and visit me tomorrow."

We went indoors. I reminded Letitia that pigs could be very unpredictable. We all were having cocoa and a night-cap when a vehicle screeched to a halt outside the farm. We had not been expecting anyone. I looked out of the window and saw a sports car. I was relieved when I saw Aaron climb out of the passenger seat, and head for the front door. I had not expected to see Aaron until Easter in a couple of weeks. The driver who I did not recognise followed him and they both burst into the house.

"Hello, Mum, hello, Dad... surprise," said Aaron. "I persuaded Charlie here to drive me ... his folks don't live too far away."

I turned to greet the other young man who was quite tall. He was maybe about 23 or 24. He had a disarming smile and a shock of black hair with a small blond streak. He put out his hand to shake hands and said,

"How do you do, Mrs Martyns?"

"How do you do, Charlie? Nice to meet you. Does your family live very far from here?"

He mentioned a town about sixty miles away which was further than not "too far away".

Aaron and Charlie readily accepted an offer of hot chocolate, toast and fruit cake. They chatted amiably and I learned more about the Honourable Charles Catton. I learned Charlie's family were rather well-heeled and he had been at public school. However, despite staying at school until he was nearly nineteen, he had not at that time performed well enough to be admitted to university. His family supported him while he re-took exams several times over at the local College of Education. He was now nearly twenty four having started the same courses as Aaron last September.

The conversation turned to Patrick White. Whereas Aaron raised his eyebrows in a similar manner to Alain and said,

"Nice try, Mum, pull the other leg," Charlie said, "Wow, cool, terrific."

Letitia yawned and said that they should meet Patrick tomorrow. She took herself off to bed. Alain cleared his throat and added,

"Well he may have to do that another time as he has a way to go to get home."

Alain and I took ourselves off to bed and left Aaron and Charlie chatting.

There was no lie-in for me on Saturday morning since I still had the animals to feed. When I came downstairs first thing leaving Alain snoring I was not surprised to find Charlie asleep on our living room settee. He was fully clothed, and one leg dangled on the floor. His mouth open slightly, and his tongue poked out. Occasionally, he murmured something in his sleep such as "Nanny more choccies" and "Nanny, nanny beddy-bise." I got the feeling Charlie was one of those people who compensated for his lack of brainpower with a sweet nature. I hoped Aaron would not take too much advantage of him.

As it was, the next morning turned out to be rather odd. Aaron was still in disbelief until Patrick started asking him questions,

"As youngest... *snort*... piglet was there much competition with your siblings...?"

Aaron and Charlie spent about two hours just chatting to Patrick about their lives. If Patrick understood anything about going to university, and student life it was unclear. However, Patrick also asked many questions about human houses, human food and music.

"This is so cool talking to you... I think I'll give my folks a miss this weekend," said Charlie.

Later, when I told Alain about our extra weekend guest he raised his eyebrows and said,

"Ah well, I suppose your pig can entertain them and keep them out of my hair."

Meanwhile, Charlie proposed to Aaron and me, "I would like to go and buy the piggie a TV... I mean you already got him a radio so I don't see why he can't have a TV."

"That is very kind," I said, "but although he can talk he is only a pig. I couldn't let you spend money like that."

"No probs," said Charlie. "The folks give me this big allowance... it would be such fun."

Before I could stop him, Charlie pulled Aaron by the sleeve out of the door, and they whizzed off in the sports car presumably to the nearest market town about fifteen miles away. They were away for a relatively short time and returned with a massive flat box squeezed into the back of the sports car.

"It's only 42 inches, I am afraid," prattled Charlie, "but I couldn't slide anything bigger behind us. I've got a voice activated remote so piggy can change his channels ... oh... and I squeezed in the boot a freebox receiver too... and a reception extender you can poke out the door."

I sat watching Charlie, Aaron and Letitia fix the TV to a bracket on the wall and fiddle about with cables and the aerial extender. Patrick munched on some pony carrots I had obtained from the animal feed outlet. He seemed intrigued by what they were doing and in between mouthfuls would ask the odd question such as,

"How is it different to radio?"

Letitia replied, "You get a picture to go with the voices."

Patrick said, "I heard a thing on the radio about a human called Marconi who invented the radio... Does it work the same way?"

"No... not quite," said Letitia.

"Enough with the science enquiries," said Aaron. "I've just about finished... let's see if we can get it to work at first with normal remote. I will set up the voice activated remote later."

He pressed a button and the screen lit up. He went through the options with Patrick looking transfixed. Eventually a programme came on screen. As it happened it was a nature programme about elephants. Patrick looked utterly astonished.

"*Grunt grunt snort,* those are huge... they are not a type of pig at all are they?" he said.

"Naw..." said Charlie. "They are elephants, of course."

"What's an elephant?" asked Patrick.

"A very big wild animal who lives in India or Africa," replied Letitia.

"Where is India? Africa?" asked Patrick.

I began to wonder what we had started by allowing him a television. It was clear it was going to take some time to setup the voice activation and teach Patrick how to use it. Aaron and Charlie said they would return next weekend and continue with the job particularly if I had no time myself.

I went to see to the other animals, including recently born piglets fathered by Patrick, and left Patrick watching television with Aaron, Charlie and Letitia. They were still there when I went into the house to start preparing an evening meal. I was pleased to see that Alain had already made a start by chopping up some onions and vegetables.

"Thank you," I said. "Everyone else is watching TV with Patrick."

Alain passed me a glass of wine and said, "Some of my contemporaries spend their weekends on the golf course or maybe playing tennis with the wife. Or the more adventurous might tell me they go hiking with their partners. Those who think they are cultured boast of evenings at the theatre. But it all sounds very pedestrian compared to what happens here. Life is never dull with you, Emmie."

Chapter 4
Patrick's Diary
Expanding my Horizons

When I started to talk to humans I was not prepared for their surprise and disbelief. I thought they would be pleased. Some humans were not at all happy to have my opinions. Emmie's mate Alain didn't visit often and when he did he always seemed to be wary of me. However, there were sufficient humans who would talk to me which was a good thing since I could never see myself just grunting and squealing with other pigs again. I had begun to realise that I was lonely and craved the company of those who could tell me more about the human world. It was only from watching television programmes that I had discovered the size and complexity of the world.

I had known for a while there were different breeds of pig and other farm animals, although until a TV programme on farming I had never seen cows or sheep before. Both seemed rather silly animals compared to pigs. I could not help wondering whether they tasted good.

As for animals such as elephants and hippos I was amazed by their size. I was pleased none lived near me. There were so many people. I grew to realise I spoke what they called English but there were many other languages. There were symbols too on the screen called 'letters'. I soon realised I needed to learn to read. Human children were taught at the piglet stage, so I needed to learn fast.

Of the humans around me I understood that Scuffy found reading quite difficult himself. He was kind to me, but I did not think he could help me with my reading. As for his sire Flemmy I was not sure that he could read at all. Alain, Emmie's mate was cautious of me and only there some of the time. I thought the youngsters probably my best bet, but I knew they only visited.

"Teach me to read. Oink," I said to Letitia who was my favourite.

She laughed. "No please?" she said. "Are you sure?"

"Yes please," I replied.

"I say, what fun," said the one called Charlie.

Aaron responded, "We are all going away again soon but we can do something. There is an old magnetic board with magnetic letters and numbers which I think is in the loft. We could try and get that down."

Sure enough this small board appeared within a short time. Letitia said,

"I've got some children's books too."

The young humans made a start in teaching me my ABC. After they had left, Emmie would spend 5 minutes teaching me when she could. It was only a matter of weeks before I could read the writing on the television.

Emmie was very tolerant of all my questions. We read some children's books together. One was about teddy bears which are not real bears which I believe to be a fierce animal, but things made of fluffy cloth and given to entertain human piglets. Another book was supposed to be about a family of pigs, but they were like no pigs I had ever met. I found there was a television show about this family too. They were rather bright colours, and they could all talk. There were other characters who were supposed to be animals too, but all the creatures were the same size. There was a hen, a cow, a dog, and an elephant who also talked. It was cheerful stuff but didn't seem to relate to real life; but I suppose it was meant for human piglets.

I learned a fair amount about human habits from the television. If humans did not live in a country where there was a war or a drought their houses tended to be quite big and comfortable. I coveted their beds. I found their bathrooms and toilets very amusing. While I understood the wish to wallow... Why, oh why, would one want to wash the dirt off? The whole point of wallowing in muddy water is that it helps cool the skin and ward off flies. As for their things called toilets, I got that one did not want to fill one's house with pooh etcetera, but I could not see why a shovel like Scuffy used would not do to clean out a corner. It seemed unnecessarily complicated.

The young humans returned at various times and would spend time with me. Once, the one called Charlie brought in a very large crate with cans of liquid. He told me it was called beer and made me promise not to tell anyone I was having some of this human drink. He poured two or three cans into my bucket. Aaron who of course was with him, and Charlie began opening some more cans and started drinking too. The liquid made me feel all warm inside. We drank all the cans in the crate between us. I found the beer made me feel quite mellow and jolly. Charlie and Aaron were laughing loudly.

Eventually when we were laughing noisily Emmie appeared. She saw the large box of empty beer cans and looked very angry.

"What on earth are you doing getting Patrick rat-arsed? How many rules have you broken?"

Aaron and Charlie giggled and slurred their words. I said,

"There are no rodents on my posterior," which they seemed to find absolutely hilarious.

Emmie said, "I meant drunk... inebriated... under the influence of alcohol."

She attempted to explain things to me.

"You will all have horrible hangovers tomorrow." She continued and looked at me, "The after-effect of imbibing a lot of alcohol is a hangover. You usually have a bad headache with a hangover."

I did have a headache the next day and I felt very sleepy. This was unfortunate since I awoke to the sound of humans shouting.

They were female voices. I could see through the open part of the doorway to my quarters two female humans who looked rather like Emmie. There was an older one with grey hair and some wrinkles around her eyes and a younger one whose voice even sounded similar to Emmie.

The older one was saying, "Well, Mathilda, is this how you treat your grandmother. Heading to see animals instead of to visit me... I have such ungrateful grandchildren. You all hardly bother with me..."

The younger one replied, "But, Gran I am home for a bit, and I was going to come over and take you out to lunch. I didn't know you would be here today. Aaron and Letitia have both given me a ridiculous story of Mum's boar being able to talk, and I wanted to see the animal before they were able to play some joke on me."

"A talking pig? Whatever next... Can't you do better than that?" railed the older one who I understood to be Emmie's mother Rebecca.

"Can't a fellow get some sleep?" I interjected.

"Who said that?" said both women.

"I did," I said grumpily. "I am the said boar, I was asleep... oink... go... oink, away."

By this time Emmie appeared.

"Mum... Mathilda... what a lovely surprise."

"You have a pig who talks," said Rebecca.

"Yes I know," said Emmie. "And he is probably nursing a headache as Aaron and his pal gave him beer. Can we go indoors?"

She ushered her mother and her eldest daughter away from me. I had my sleep but they all returned a few hours later.

"You can talk then?" Rebecca said loudly as she peered through the open part of the doorway.

"I can talk. And I can hear too," I responded. "There is no need to shout at me as if I was deaf."

"Why are you talking?" asked Mathilda.

"Why shouldn't I?" I replied testily. "Why are you talking?"

"Because I can," she said.

"Likewise," I responded.

Mathilda looked at her mother, "Does Dad know?"

"Of course," replied Emmie.

Mathilda went on, "Well, Mum, I suggest you don't broadcast it. I have a legal career to pursue. I don't want to be associated with well... A funny farm."

Emmie responded, "You always have called it a 'funny farm'."

I could see Mathilda pulling a face. Rebecca said,

"Well, I am going to enjoy talking to Patrick, if he has no objections?"

"I have no objections, but I do wish you would include me in your conversation," I said. "You can chat to me unless I tell you I want to be left alone to take a nap... or I am eating or watching television. I have some programmes about wildlife in Africa I really like to watch... I particularly like elephants."

"You sound like a typical bloke!" said Rebecca. "I will come back another day quite soon and bring you some of those pony carrots that Em has stashed away... we can have a proper natter then."

"Can't you bring me beer?" I asked more in hope than expectation.

"I know the rules," said Rebecca. "No human food, no getting you drunk!"

I was beginning to understand that humans had far too many rules and that also rules were often there to be broken. I wondered who I could persuade to bring me more of that beer and if they could also be persuaded to bring me human food.

Mathilda did not come and visit for quite some time, but Rebecca returned quite quickly. She let herself into my quarters. She had a folding chair with her and a large bag. I grunted a "hello" and she sat down. Out of her bag she brought out a container and said,

"Hope you don't mind but I've brought a thermos of coffee with me?"

"No beer?" I asked. She shook her head and poured some dark brown fluid into a mug. I sniffed and said, "Doesn't smell like my sort of thing anyway." I thought about the delights of beer and wished I might have some more.

Then she took out a large carrot and offered it to me. I grabbed it from her hand and munched it up. Trying not to sound too greedy I said,

"Thank you... oink... I wouldn't mind more but only if you have some."

"I can do better than just carrots," said Rebecca. "A farmer friend of mine lifted the last of his swedes a bit on the late side and most of them are too misshapen to sell, so when I go, I can leave you with some lovely big swedes... Here is one to try!"

She handed one to me. I was careful not to bite her fingers which being a pig was quite unusual I gather. Most pigs are not known for their table manners. The swede was nice and firm and crunchy, and made a real change. I felt the juice run down my chops as I chomped away.

"That's... oink... really good," I said.

"Now, Patrick," said Rebecca, "I've been around farming a long time but never met a talking pig before you. I was just wondering what sets you apart from other pigs?"

I gave it some thought.

"I know I am different in many ways to other pigs, but I don't know why," I responded. "I don't wish to be a human, but I quite like human things."

"Do you mind pigs being made into sausages?" queried Rebecca.

"Well I don't want to be made into sausages," I said. "But I wouldn't mind eating some."

"But that's eating other pigs," she said. I replied making it clear that it was fine as long as I didn't have to try to make the sausages because that was beyond me and my trotters.

"I mean," I said, trying to explain, "if you died suddenly here and I was very very hungry, I might eat you... but that is not likely as Emmie keeps me well fed."

Rebecca laughed. "I am glad she does," she replied.

"What do you think of the humans you are meeting?" she continued.

I tried to explain how puzzling and contradictory I found humankind but that there were quite a few who made me feel almost protective, like sows are with their piglets.

"I think these ones are my main friends," I said. Then I found myself grunting and thinking about the bag of swedes.

"Are you my friend?" asked Rebecca.

"Yes," I replied. "Especially if you give me some of those swedes."

She poured out the remaining Swedes for me before she left. After that occasion I enjoyed regular visits from Rebecca. She usually sat down with her flask of coffee and brought me swedes and carrots. One day she said,

"Carrots and swedes are all gone... but I have been very naughty and bought you something from the supermarket."

"I don't suppose it's some beer?" I asked. I had a rough idea what a supermarket was from watching television. They had many things for human to eat and drink. I envied humans the variety of foodstuffs. I didn't like the sound of their cleaning and washing stuffs. I was also puzzled as to how one would navigate around these places since they were frequently full of people dancing and singing from what I saw on television.

She shook her head and took a big bag of apples out of her usual bag.

"Apples!"

Well, I was pretty happy with this. I had only had apples about twice before in my life. I grunted with pleasure. It did not take me long to finish off the apples after we had concluded our chat. That juice! That munchiness! Oh, for a meal which was mainly apples and swedes washed down with plenty of beer.

I was also very happy when Aaron and Charlie turned up again. I grunted happy greetings and asked if they had any more beer.

"We'll sneak some in later," said Charlie, "but I've got something more important... I have brought you something called a laptop. I am going to hook you up to the house internet and the voice controls... then you can surf the internet!"

"Surf the internet?" I asked. "Is that something to do with swimming in big waves? There isn't enough water here, and I am not sure I would like it."

Aaron did his best to explain things to me. It sounded very intriguing, and it sounded as if I might need the reading skills I was developing.

Emmie came out to check what Charlie and Aaron were doing. I think she was suspicious they might bring me beer. She stood with her arms folded,

"Are you sure this is wise?" she asked. "There is a lot of crazy stuff on the internet."

I grunted and said, "I don't want to... oink, upset you, Em, you've been so good to me."

She replied,

"There is a lot of scary and untrue stuff out there, Patrick. I was more concerned about you."

Charlie gave me a big beaming smile,

"For now I'll just try to show him how to get some music which he likes... there was some classical stuff, Aaron?"

Aaron nodded, "We'll show him how to get some music played by the Royal Philharmonic Orchestra."

The reality was they also showed me how to access music by James Brown, Herbie Hancock, Tina Turner and Diana Ross and the like. When Em was busy indoors they also brought in another crate of beer. Charlie, Aaron and I sat enjoying our cans of beer, but Aaron would not let me have the music turned up loud as I wanted.

"Shhh," he said, "Mum mustn't hear us... or she might come back and make a fuss. As for Dad he would be furious."

Charlie got a small pouch out of his pocket and a container with some little white bits of paper. He put some brown stuff in the paper.

"Fancy a ciggy, Aaron?" he said. "It's alright... it's not wacky baccy!"

"You know I don't usually smoke, it doesn't really go with keeping fit for my sports," said Aaron as Charlie lit the end of the little white paper tube with a little device he had taken from his pocket. He started sucking it and blowing out some smoke. "Go on..." he said. "Maybe the piggy would like to try a ciggy too!"

"OK... just this once," said Aaron. He soon was blowing smoke like Charlie. It was all very puzzling. Charlie also made what they called a cigarette for me and offered it to me. I tried to eat it, but it didn't taste very nice, so I spat it out. Their smoke made me cough a little.

"I think we should stop with the smoking, Charlie," said Aaron.

I grunted, "Oink, I agree." Charlie looked a little sad but was soon placated with another can of beer.

After a while, the beer was finished. This time they took the empty cans with them so that Em would not find them in my quarters.

She came to say "Goodnight" to me. I was listening to the orchestra playing Mussorgsky's 'Pictures from an Exhibition'.

She wrinkled her nose, "I smell smoke."

"I don't smell anything," I said falsely and quickly changed the subject. "These orchestra things are so clever... oink, oink... I shall use the internet to find out more about how they make the music."

Emmie smiled and said that she was off to bed.

The music played at a low level and the night was still. I couldn't sleep. I decided to change the music to James Brown. I turned it up a little, grunting loudly at the voice controls, then some more. Then I tried what humans called dancing. I was really enjoying snorting and moving to 'Get Up (I feel like being a Sex Machine)' when a loud voice bellowed,

"Shut up and turn that bloody music off... you, you over-sized joint of pork."

There stood Emmie's mate Alain, very red in the face, dressed in a striped outfit which I understand humans call pyjamas. I seemed to have upset him.

Chapter 5

A hot summer

The weather had become very warm, and it seemed we were having a sizzling summer. Mathilda, Letitia and Aaron had finished their summer exams and no doubt there would be tension while they awaited their results.

I had confidence in all of them. I was sure Mathilda would soon shine as a pupil barrister, Letitia would grapple with the final year of her degree and Aaron would sail through to his second year. I had a feeling that his friend Charlie would be retaking his first year. I liked Charlie but I could not help thinking he was a bad influence on Aaron. Fortunately, we would not be seeing him for a few weeks. It appeared Charlie had fallen head over heels in love with a Swedish exchange student and had followed her back to Stockholm after his exams.

Immediately after his exams Aaron came home. Alain had arranged to take a couple of weeks off at that time. They spent the first week sailing at the reservoir and managed a quick week down to the south of France where one of Clothilde's friends keeps a yacht. They flew to a regional airport so that they could immediately access the coast and did not visit Clothilde and Harry.

Mathilda spent some time at the farm at this time, mostly on a deckchair in the garden with a cold drink. She mainly ignored Patrick unlike Letitia who when she came home after her exams went to see Patrick almost as soon as she arrived. Apart from that Letitia was pleased to have some part-time work helping me with my legal business.

"Isn't it hot?" she said. "You poor thing cooped up indoors."

"But at least *snort* I can't get sunburn," replied Patrick. "But I do miss a good wallow… I do wish now I had a bathroom like you humans have."

His remarks gave me food for thought. I had not envisaged making use of his services with the sows again until about September, even before I found out he could speak. I had not thought about the hot conditions. I spoke to Scuffy and Flemmy about it.

"I think we'll have to hose 'im down from time to time. You got a tap in that there shed," said Flemmy. "I know he's got telly and radio and whatnot, so we'll have to keep water away."

"How about a child's paddling pool?" asked Scuffy.

"He'd squash sides down and might splash water near the 'lectrics," said Flemmy.

"What if we put some screening in front of whatever we got to stop splashes?" I asked. "I am not sure about a paddling pool either."

Flemmy replied, "Well when you've made your mind up I've got some old boarding I could shove up."

I told Letitia about the discussion.

"What you need is an old large bath," she said. "Or even a jacuzzi!"

I looked at all the adverts on social media and second-hand

websites. It was not going to be easy. Eventually I saw an ad which read,

'Extra-large corner bath free for collection. Disposal due to refurbishment'.

There was a picture too of a hideous orange bath. No wonder the owner wanted to refurbish his bathroom.

I contacted the owner and went with Scuffy to collect it in a trailer.

"I suppose it might make an animal trough for your farm," he said.

"Something like that…" I responded. I felt the seller of the bath would hardly believe the real reason for its purchase.

Flemmy and Scuffy managed to secure some boards from the ceiling beams to prevent splashes coming out from the corner of the brick shed where the bath was to be placed, bolted in one corner to the wall but standing on bricks. A debate ensued about whether to block up the plughole or let it be drained by pulling out the plug.

"Although we'll 'ave to fill it with a hose, I reckon I can fix an outlet pipe to the bath and attach it to a bit of old tubing which can be pushed through the wall… the main issue about the plughole is whether the pig would knock the plug out," said Flemmy.

"*Snort snort,* if you point out this feature to me," said Patrick, "I am sure I can be very careful."

Patrick watched as his bathing quarter took shape. If a pig could be said to be smiling, he could be said to be smiling ear to ear.

One very hot afternoon his 'bathroom' was finished. Scuffy filled the old bath halfway with water.

"Aren't you going to fill it all the way up?" queried Patrick.

"Naw, when you get in it, your weight will make the water come near the top anyway."

"My *snort* weight?" Patrick looked annoyed so I tried explaining it to him.

"Be careful also, Patrick, not to knock the bricks," I said.

"I am, *snort snort,* a very careful pig," he said.

Fortunately, the bath was low enough that he could step into it. Soon a very contented pig was wallowing in an orange bath.

"Can I have some music?" he asked.

"Classical or something funky?" I replied.

"*Snort snort,* maybe some Brahms," he replied.

I pondered the situation. Patrick was picking up more human tastes every day and was really quite spoiled. In the meantime, life went on. I had legal work to do. My clientele was increasing. I seem to have developed a niche practice in wills for the agricultural community and what I would describe as 'farming' litigation.

Jim Birkshaw had found himself being sued by the animal rights' protestors for compensation for their injuries. It seemed his insurance company was being difficult. They wanted to settle the claims even though Jim felt he had done nothing wrong. It was not just that he would have to shell out for £2,500 which was his excess, but he was aware his premiums would go up and felt it was an invitation to others to make spurious claims. He told me that the insurance company just wanted the matter to go away quietly but he wanted to fight it. I was able to negotiate a position with them that if Jim contested the court action and won, the insurers would not put up his premiums. They would also contribute 50% of any legal costs he did not recover from the activists.

On one of Jim's visits to the farm to discuss his case he said,

"I've been hearing rumours that boar I sold you can talk… you don't want animal rights' people bothering you over such a silly rumour."

"It's true," I said.

"Nice joke, Emmie," he replied.

I took him round to the brick shed and said,

"Patrick, do you remember Jim? He is visiting, can you say 'hello'?"

Patrick was wallowing in his bath at the time. Some Debussy was playing gently in the background. Some slight splashing could be heard but he was mainly obscured by the screening.

"*Oink oink* hello. You are not going to move me I hope?" came Patrick's comment.

"Nice one, Emmie," said Jim. "Clever trick."

"It's no trick, come round the screen," I said.

Jim peered around it. Patrick was lying on his back with his trotters upwards in an almost human pose.

"I don't wish to be moved," he said. "I enjoy my comforts."

"Bloody hell!" said Jim. "His mouth is moving."

"Of course my mouth is moving," said Patrick, "I'm talking to you."

"Pardon?" said Jim looking increasingly shocked.

"I said I was talking to you, and I don't want to be moved, *oink oink*," said Patrick.

"No one is moving you," I said. Patrick grunted.

"Emmie, have you something strong to drink?" said a rather pale looking Jim.

Rebecca had just turned up, so we took Jim into the house and sat him down and gave him some brandy. He seemed to recover after a bit.

"He really can talk," he said to me. "But I do hope the rest of them can't."

I reassured him that as far as I knew Patrick was quite unique. We spent some time talking about his legal case while Rebecca chatted to Patrick.

"I've always done my best to apply a high animal welfare standard," said Jim. "Yet they are trying to suggest that my pigs' conditions made them savage. It's not true… my pigs are kept with as much room as is feasible. I don't use that awful crate system. I really don't understand why they picked on me."

I tried to reassure him.

Soon, Alain and Aaron came back from their trip. Alain went to London for a week to sort out some cases which couldn't wait. My three children lazed around the farm and Patrick lazed in his bath in the hot weather. I knew that when Alain came back, we would be off to see his parents in France. Mathilda agreed to join us for the trip, which would be for about a fortnight. We tended to take the journey to their house in Provence slowly, taking about 3 days there and 3 days back. If truth be told I could not stand staying with my mother-in-law for more than a week.

For part of the time I was away, Aaron was going to a sports' training camp, and I was relieved Charlie would not be there. However, for about 8 or 9 days he would be at the farm, and it was always possible Charlie might turn up. Whilst Letitia would be staying at the farm, I was not sure she could keep Aaron and Charlie from doing something undesirable like getting Patrick drunk. Letitia would also be keeping an eye on my legal business; although I was taking my work phone with me it was good to have her back home as well. I knew many people would be away on holiday, but I could not rule out something happening with my work. I felt it was time to bring in reinforcements, so I pleaded with my mother Rebecca to come and stay.

She no longer had a farm of her own to run but she did have a red-setter dog called Selwyn, Pickle and Tickle her tabby cats, half a dozen hens and a nanny goat called Maude. She fortunately did not have any Parish Council meetings at that time. She was fortunately quite co-operative.

"It's a good thing your mut Piecrust and Selwyn are good friends because I will have to bring him… I can just pop back for an hour or two here and there for the rest of my creatures," she said.

It was true the two dogs got on very well.

"I shall enjoy spending time with that pig Patrick, so you go and enjoy your holiday."

As it turned out I think my mother had a much better time than me.

A visit to France.

It was very hot driving through France and when we arrived at Clothilde and Harry's house I felt worn out, crumpled and frazzled.

"Can I 'elp you find a change of clothes and maybe give you some perfume?" was the initial jibe.

We had agreed not to tell her about Patrick. It was already bad enough that she was constantly needling me about my little farm and how she thought it was bad for Alain. Later in the day she added,

"When you go 'ome to your goats or whatever it is… you should give thought to Alain's reputation."

I responded, "I don't think Alain's reputation is in any way affected by his wife keeping animals."

She persisted, "If you go to ze social functions, it is not good if your wife smells like a farmyard."

I resisted the urge to be sarcastic and to tell her I went to legal functions in Wellingtons' and an old pair of overalls chewing a piece of straw and saying "Ooh aar".

"It is not good for my grandchildren," she continued, "to 'ave a mother who is... how do you say… such a peasant."

At that stage Mathilda weighed into my defence,

"Grand-maman, I know my mother does not wear her casual

farming clothes to court or out to dinner… and also your reference to 'peasants' is very classist!"

Clothilde looked furious. "I 'ope you will not catch these agricultural ways from your maman… you looked nearly as bad as 'er when you arrived."

Mathilda looked furious and I was concerned that a full-scale argument was going to break out.

"Clothilde. We travelled a long way so that we could see Harry and yourself. That is why we were not dressed in our best things. We would like to take Harry and you out during our trip... to a restaurant of your choosing, so I promise you, we will dress up."

It was not as if everything was perfect in Clothilde's household. She had a little Bichon Frise with unsavoury habits who had not improved since last we visited Clothilde and Harry. Bijoux seemed no jewel to me. Now and again, he would quietly raise his leg on the coffee table. At mealtime Clothilde would lift him onto the dining room table and let him share her dinner plate. He really did not like Alain and several times had tried to sink his teeth in Alain's ankle, only to be deterred by Alain's smart leather ankle boots. It appeared he was very jealous of Alain. Harry seemed not to notice any of this. Retirement had so relaxed him that any apparent difficulties on any front seemed completely to pass him by. If Harry could have been any more laid back he would have been comatose.

When we did indeed go out to dinner to a rather nice brasserie, Bijoux came too. He was placed on the table, and no-one batted an eyelid. Pierre the chef came out of the kitchen and greeted everyone warmly. He kissed Clothilde on both cheeks and gave Bijoux a porcelain saucer of chopped up raw steak.

While I toyed with my bouillabaisse, I could not help envying my mother Rebecca back at the farm.

After dinner out I quietly rang her when I was sipping a cold drink in Clothilde's garden.

"How are things?"

"It's all fine," she said. "Aaron has Charlie visiting him now, but I am keeping a careful eye on them. I think they have spent the evening at the pub."

"And Letitia... and Patrick?" I asked.

"Letitia is sitting with Patrick as we speak," she replied.

"If you are not too far from them could you put them on the phone?" I enquired.

There was a pause for half a minute.

"You are on speaker phone," said Rebecca.

"Hello, everyone," I said.

"Hello, Mum," said Letitia. "How is the grand mere?"

Letitia had never been close to her grandmother.

"Don't ask," I said. "Let's just say I will be glad to be home. Even Dad is not having a wonderful time. That little dog she has keeps trying to bite him."

"Well everything is fine here although it's still rather hot," continued Letitia. "Charlie is here but no fun and games from Aaron and him as yet."

"*Snort snort,* more's the pity," came Patrick's voice. "I wish they would bring me beer."

"How are you, Patrick?" I asked.

"I am alright. When are you, *snort,* coming back? It's not the same hearing your voice on that phone thing, *oink oink,*" was the reply.

"Soon, I will be home soon, Patrick," I said, shortly before ending the call with my mother.

Clothilde had walked out into the garden just at the end of my call.

"Who is Patrick?" she queried. "'ave you taken a lover?"

"Of course not," I said. "It is just a friend of the children."

"I will ask Alain," she said ominously. I crossed my fingers he would say the same thing.

Fortunately, his reply was even better.

"Just some needy friend of Letitia," he said. "Stop stirring it, Maman."

Clothilde looked crestfallen and no further enquiry was made about Patrick. Harry appeared not to notice the tensions and just offered more cold drinks or wine as if nothing untoward had been said.

Soon enough we were driving back through rural France towards the ferry port. I had two days of watching the countryside go by as Alain drove. We stopped at a couple of pleasant auberge. My short period of relaxation was then interrupted by a call from Rebecca.

"I thought you should know," she said, "I've had a girl from the local newspaper sniffing around. She had heard a rumour about a talking pig. I am not sure the source of her information."

"Oh, dear," I said. "You will have to stall her until I have thought of a strategy."

Rebecca replied, "I think it's okay for now, because I said she needed to speak to you on your return. I've also told Letitia and the boys not to say anything to her and not to let her in. Shall I mention it to Patrick?"

"Yes," I said. "Please ask Patrick not to speak to anyone he doesn't know."

The conversation ended. I really did not know what the effect would be if there was press attention. I did not fancy TV crews and cranks camped out, outside my home. I would have to come up with a plan.

Chapter 6

Humans get very excited.

*T*hat farmer Jim seemed very shocked and surprised when I first spoke to him. Hadn't he realised I was a cut above other pigs? Emmie had to give him something called a brandy. I understood that had strong alcohol in it. Beer had alcohol in it. I pondered why I could not try brandy; it sounded like something I would like.

Rebecca seemed a calm person. I did not mind too much that she was left in charge while Emmie, Alain and Mathilda went to that place called France, although I would have preferred if Emmie had been around as well. Aaron and Charlie were there. Rebecca made it quite hard for them to give me beer, but they did slip a few cans into me. I watched less television in the hot weather and wallowed for much of the time in the bath they had given me listening to classical music.

One day Rebecca came and spoke to me and seemed rather worried.

"A reporter has been asking about the talking pig," she said.

"Am I... oink... going to be famous?" I asked.

"I hope not," said Rebecca. "We don't want people trying to take you away from here to examine you."

I saw her point.

Soon Emmie came back from France. She complained about something called a Clothilde. I don't think she had a good time. Emmie, Rebecca and Letitia all gathered round me to discuss matters. Scuffy, Aaron and Charlie hovered about in the background.

"I think," said Letitia, "if we give her a little bit of what she wants the reporter might go away."

"How do you mean?" said Emmie.

"Well, if she met Patrick briefly, and he just said the odd word... very grunty... she might think it was just a question of sounds that sounded like talking... as if someone had taught him to copy a few sounds," replied Letitia.

"That sounds very dull," I said, "I am very proud of my intellect," and I tried not to grunt too much.

"It's meant to be dull," said Letitia.

"I get it," said Aaron, "perhaps 'hello' and 'bye-bye' and a line of a nursery rhyme."

I was yet to be convinced.

"Won't this person realise I am a very clever pig?" I asked.

"Not if you act stupid like people expect," said Aaron.

Rebecca said she would go through some nursery rhymes with me. She managed to put them on screen. I was able to impress her with my reading skills.

"Twinkle, twinkle little star, how I wonder what you are..." I couldn't help grunting and laughing. We tried again,

"Ride a cock horse to Banbury cross to see a fine lady ride on a fine horse, with rings on her fingers," I started laughing as Rebecca sang, "and bells on her toes, she shall have music wherever she goes."

I laughed and grunted and laughed. It was too ridiculous. I rolled about grunting and laughing.

Soon she tried something called 'Old Macdonald' and we were able to work something out. We had a plan. I wouldn't say I was happy with it, but it was something I was prepared to do.

Emmie said she would phone the reporter. A female came who only looked a little older than Mathilda, although I am no great judge of human ages. She had glasses and a notebook but took her phone out and asked if she could film and record things if the opportunity arose.

Emmie said to me, "Now, Patrick be a good pig and say hello." There was a twinkle in her eye and a smirk on her face, so I obligingly went, "Grunt-grunt," in a manner that sounded slightly like, "Hello".

"Now I am going to sing," said Emmie, and began singing 'Old Macdonald'.

"Old Macdonald had a farm," she sung, and I joined in with a, "squeal... oh... squeal oh... squeal... ohhh."

She continued, "On that farm he had a pig," and I did my, "squeal... oh," bit. Then she said

"Here a..." I obligingly grunted, "There a..."

It was quite a performance if I say so myself. It seemed to satisfy the reporter who went off with a smile on her face.

Emmie saw her off the premises and came back to me.

"That went well," she said, "our singing was quite impressive," she laughed.

"Well it was hardly Wagner's Meistersingers' or the Motown Greats!" I replied with a grunt. "If it leaves me in peace, then that's what is required."

Over the next few days, it remained hot, and I enjoyed my bath. Rebecca brought me summer fruits and Aaron and Charlie secretly gave me beer.

Alain had not until recently had much to do with me. Recently, he had taken to chatting to me late in the evening after dinner, often with something humans called a 'Scotch' in his hand. He let me sniff his glass once. At first I didn't like the smell and winced.

That made him laugh. Then I said,

"It's interesting. It smells of earth and bonfires and thistles. Can I try it?"

He said,

"I know about your beer habit, pig, so I am not going to introduce you to 15-year-old Scotch."

I grunted and said, "Oh. Pity, I would have liked to try some. My name is Patrick by the way, not pig. I don't suppose you could arrange for me to try some wine? I might like that."

"I don't think so, pig. You are enough trouble as it is."

"Me? Trouble? I don't think so," I responded.

"I don't suppose you can help it," Alain continued, "but it would have been a whole lot simpler if you had just been a normal pig rather than a talking one."

I did agree with him to some extent.

And so, summer went by quickly. After their holiday in France, Emmie and Alain resumed what they called their 'cases', although it seemed they were less busy with them. Emmie said that it was still 'the holiday season'. Sometimes she chatted about what she was doing. I didn't always understand what she was on about.

"Sorry," she said, one evening, "I haven't really seen you for the last couple of days. I was getting an injunction to prevent some nasty new neighbours pulling down old Mrs Cuthbottom's hedge. Her cottage has been there four hundred years. It's an ancient yew hedge so may have been there as long as the cottage. The new people are townies... they wanted to open up their frontage and make it wider."

"Wouldn't that be very uncomfortable?" I asked, not understanding.

Emmie explained it to me. Humans seemed to do the oddest things. There was a row of old cottages with gardens. The new people wanted to get rid of their garden and cover it with concrete to park their cars. It seemed they already had something called a garage for their cars up a driveway to the side, but they wanted to see their cars at the front rather than the cottage garden. Why move to a place if you wanted to change everything about it? I mean I could understand if they wanted a big bath like mine but getting rid of the nice greenery, what a shame!

Soon it was time for Aaron and Letitia to prepare to go back to their studies (this studying thing seemed to involve being with other young humans and going to a lot of parties). Mathilda was apparently already busy with something called a pupillage. Aaron, Letitia, Charlie, Rebecca, Emmie and I had something of a party of our own. We had apples and pears, gooseberries and currants. I had carrots and beets and the humans had something called pasties which I must admit looked most appealing. There was beer too, and we had music. Scuffy and Flemmy were there too.

Charlie and Aaron said in slurred tones how much they would miss me. Letitia kept putting her arms round me and hugging me. Eventually, Alain came out of the house and joined us, but soon the party was over.

Next day it was quite quiet. I think the young humans were enjoying what they called a 'lie in', while they still could. Alain had gone off early. He said he had a train to catch. I don't know what animal that is.

Scuffy and Flemmy came to speak to me.

"We are going to bring you a sow to visit, so you can have your wicked way!" said Flemmy.

"But you must be good and let 'er go afterwards."

I was good! Suffice it to say I did the necessary and over the next few days three more sows visited in turn. Being something of a gentleman pig I will leave it to the imagination what transpired. I had some regrets in letting each one go, but after the necessary activity I was tired. Also, I found I had little in common with them. They could not discuss music or television with me. Attracted as I was to them, they were just sows. I suppose I would not have said no to visits by sows most days, but it was good while it lasted.

Emmie seemed pleased with my efforts. However, she seemed less happy about Jim Birkshaw's case. He came to discuss developments with her. There had been something called a 'directions hearing'. They had been discussing it in the house, but stepped outside so they could visit me.

"I really don't know what the judge was playing at," Emmie was saying. "There were perfectly straightforward Fast Track directions and a trial window late February... early March, but this Deputy District Judge seemed very inexperienced. He allowed the claimants an application to put in a report from an animal behaviour expert, but he hasn't changed the timetable or the allocation..."

"I gather he said we could have our own expert report," said Jim.

"Yes," said Emmie, "but that would be very expensive... and there is a time limit too. We would need an expert report on pig behaviour in just over five weeks."

I grunted and wondered if I could help.

"So," said Jim, "we need a report from someone who knows pigs to say pigs behave as pigs... I am a pig farmer, isn't my word good enough?"

"Apparently not," said Emmie.

"Well what about statements from my staff?" said Jim.

"No," said Emmie. "By expert report, they mean someone who can report as an independent expert on pigs."

"Can I help?" I asked. "I am a pig so I can talk about pigs."

Jim and Emmie didn't take much notice of my comment and kept talking to each other. Emmie raised the issue of doing something called an 'appeal' but Jim did not sound very keen.

"Look," said Jim, "I must dash, I am due at my accountants' in half an hour. Please try to find a cheap solution for me. I'll be back the day after tomorrow, if that is okay?"

As it transpired the next day was very busy and I don't think Emmie had time to work out what to do about Jim's case.

There was a commotion outside the farm not long after I had my breakfast. Emmie's mobile phone rang, and I could hear her talking.

"Yes," I heard her say, "I do have the pig the local paper reporter saw…What? You are here now? Just give me five minutes."

She came and spoke to me.

"Some TV reporters from 'Northern Look' are here and want to film you."

"I've seen that TV programme. It is about local things after the News," I replied with a grunt. I added, "I suppose you don't want me to seem too clever?"

She nodded. "Yes."

"How about we do 'Old Macdonald' again," I suggested. "I could also do some Disco Grunting…"

"How do you mean?" said Emmie.

"Just put on 'Stayin' Alive' by the Bee Gees and I will squeal to it," I said.

"Are you sure?" said Emmie. I said I was.

She went away and came back later with three men. I learned

afterwards that one was the news reporter. A man holding a long black fuzzy thing was in charge of sound, and the man holding a big black box was the cameraman.

The reporter asked if he could stand in the entrance to my quarters and then said, "Action."

Emmie said, in a very condescending way,

"Hello, Patrick, we have visitors, shall we sing together?"

We did a performance of 'Old Macdonald'. Then Emmie said,

"Shall I put your music on, Patrick piggy?" It was so condescending, that in other circumstances I would have spat at her.

She switched on 'Stayin' Alive', and I squealed in what I thought were the right places.

"Oink, oink, oink... Stayin' alive."

Once the music had finished the reporter turned to camera, "Well, he wouldn't win a talent contest! But this is Northern Look reporting from a local farm with Patrick the disco pig."

After that, the men thanked Emmie very much and left.

It was not until the following evening that a piece about me appeared on television on Northern Look. The host of the programme introduced it.

"Some regions have talking dogs; some places have performing parrots. Well, I am pleased to say our area has its very own singing and dancing pig," he said.

Then they played some film with my disco dance. I seemed as porcine as you would have expected. There was no inkling of how clever I am. I understood later from Aaron and Charlie that the film of me singing and dancing became a great favourite on social media.

Next morning, Emmie was talking to Scuffy.

"That pig's dancing caused a right laugh with my mates at the pub," he said.

"Well I hope you played the whole thing down," said Emmie.

"I am not 'that pig', I am called Patrick," I reminded Scuffy.

"Okay, mate!" he replied.

I understood humans used the expression 'mate' for a pal or a friend, so I grunted my approval.

Later in the day Jim arrived. Jim and Emmie came to see me. Jim seemed to enjoy the distraction from his court case. He was talking to Emmie.

"These wretched people have presumably found their own tame expert to say the conditions for my pigs are wrong," said Jim. "The blasted insurance company are not paying for things at the moment... and the people you have found Emmie either can't help in the timescale, or want a ridiculous amount of money... and we don't even know what they will say... Do we have to have an expert report on pig behaviour?"

"We don't have to..." said Emmie, "but you might be at a disadvantage without a report, depending on the quality of their report. It should not be this hard to find an expert on pigs to say the conditions at your farm were fine..."

"I could do it," I said, "I did tell you before."

"That's a nice offer, Patrick, but how would you write a statement?" said Emmie.

"You are not taking me seriously. Charlie set up some voice recognition stuff. I already was concerned I did not have a chance to use it. In fact, I was wondering whether you could sort me out an email address so I could keep in touch with him and the family...oink," I replied.

"What could be better than a pig giving a statement about pigs!" said Jim laughing, but not sounding as if he understood I was serious.

"Patrick," said Emmie, "it is a very kind idea, but there are rules about instructing experts. Your views have to be independent..."

"Oink... they would be," I replied.

"There would have to be a letter of instruction," continued Emmie who still sounded like she treated the matter as a joke.

"As long as you displayed it on the screen I could read it and follow it," I said.

"If your report differed from the other side's report, you might have to attend court and give evidence," said Emmie. "Even if you just made a statement to say you had been a happy pig at Jim's farm someone might want to ask questions in court."

I was not sure about this 'attending court' but I knew Emmie did it, and she was not made into sausages. She returned home each time.

Alain was often in court.

These days so was Mathilda.

"You know," said Jim, "as crazy as it sounds I would not mind having something from Patrick. He started his life at my farm. He has no complaints about it. If need be, photos or a video or something could be produced to the judge."

"If expert reports cannot be agreed, usually the expert has to give evidence, now and then by video link but generally by the expert coming to court," said Emmie. "But why are we even talking about Patrick coming to court? This all sounds mad."

"Think about it," said Jim. "The effect of an actual pig saying things were okay at my farm... they would all be gob-smacked."

I grunted loudly. "I'll do it. I'll do it," I said. "I will do this report thing and you can take me in a trailer to this court place."

"It's an insane plan," said Emmie. "You will need to sign something to say that you take the risk for this idea. I hope we don't have to produce Patrick at the court... if that did happen you would need to take full responsibility for him. Hopefully, however, with modern tech, we can avoid that situation."

"Look," said Jim, "us farmers have been getting a raw deal. So for once in my otherwise sensible life I am going to try something daring."

I replied, "Well, I am only too pleased to help, oink."

Chapter 7

Preparing the expert report

I thought Jim Birkshaw must have had some sort of breakdown to want a report from Patrick, but as he was the client, I had to follow my instructions. Time was scarce. I found myself asking Charlie to visit so that we could load material onto the laptop for Patrick to read. Most material was in online form. Some material had to be scanned into the laptop. The laptop was connected to the larger television screen so that Patrick had clear visibility. Additionally, I had electronic versions of the case papers.

The worst thing was explaining to Patrick about how courts worked, and also the Civil Procedure Rules.

It was a good thing Alain was away for several days. He would have been appalled at what I was doing. I suppose he might have been interested about our discussions about courts. Patrick grunted a lot and looked as thoughtful as a pig could look.

"So," he said, "there are people called judges who were lawyers who are supposed to be clever people and they decide things when people have an argument and send writings about it to places called courts?"

"That's right," I confirmed.

"If someone has done something very bad it's the police who start the writings… and the judge is helped by 12 people called the jury. If the jury find the person did the wrong thing the judge can lock them up in a place called prison, which sounds to me like a giant nasty pig-shed, but this argument is not from the police?"

"Yes, that's right. People are claiming money from Jim, and he is claiming some money back because a sow aborted," I replied.

"If I had a bad argument with a boar," he said, "we would probably try to fight to the death, so I suppose it is a better way, provided this judge person is clever enough."

I had the job of giving Patrick an overview of the Civil Procedure Rules 1998 which are the rules and code of conduct governing procedure in the courts in England and Wales. There is a section dealing specifically with the conduct and duties of experts. I could hardly believe I was explaining this to a pig. In fact, Patrick took the whole process seriously. He appeared to read all the material carefully. He made a number of practice attempts with the voice activated software to produce written material. Along the way he noticed there was a statement from the vet who examined him some months ago.

"Why couldn't he be the expert?" he asked. "It would have been easier for you."

"He doesn't want to be caught up in an argument about porcine behaviour," I said. "He was only prepared to give a factual statement about what pigs he had treated at the farm. And any injuries or ailments."

Alain did come back for a period in the middle of the time Patrick was reading and preparing material. I felt rather guilty that I kept what we were doing from him. At last Patrick's report was ready; just in time to be exchanged with the claimants' expert report.

When I received it, it seemed the report of the claimants' expert was about as questionable as a report from a pig. Dr Clive Mettange appeared to have a Doctorate in Anthropology from an obscure university. He was closely affiliated to animal rights' and climate change activist movements. He had written articles in the past calling for farm animals to be freed and for them to be no longer kept, even if it meant farm animals actually became extinct. His 'expert' report made no comments on the facts in the case, but just repeated his point of view over farm animals.

There was a direction of the court for the experts to meet and discuss their reports to see if there was common ground, and thus avoid attending court. I had been dreading inviting some professor to meet a pig. In the event I need not have worried. I tried to arrange a telephone conference for the experts. In the event I was sharply rebuffed by the claimants' solicitors, who indicated they had been told that Dr Mettange could see nothing he wanted to discuss with Mr White. They suggested we agree by consent that each side could put written questions if they wished to the other side's expert. I readily agreed.

Patrick was easily able to fend off most of the questions. The only one he skirted around was one questioning his independence due to his past residence at the defendant's property. Little did the claimants' solicitors realise but they were asking questions of a pig. The questions I put to Dr Mettange focused on his lack of experience with pigs. His eventual reply was to the effect he did not see the need to have any actual experience with pigs. I remained concerned, however, that we would be placed in a hugely difficult position if there was an insistence on producing our expert witness in court.

Alain was home for a spell now. He worked remotely from his study and had a couple of court appearances in courts in commuting distance from home. Our work was separate and bound by client confidentiality unless I instructed him as counsel in a case or we were doing something in the public domain. Patrick did not know about client confidentiality, and I had not foreseen the need to explain it to him. Goodness knows I had explained enough to him.

Late one evening Alain went outside with a Scotch, to enjoy a breath of air and say "Hello" to Patrick before we went to bed. I was just tidying up and pouring myself a late-night glass of bramble liqueur, so I followed on some fifteen minutes after Alain. I had not thought to say to Patrick that he should not discuss Jim's case or show Alain his statement. By the time I arrived Patrick had apparently told Alain that he was Jim's expert witness on pigs and had put his statement up on the screen.

There is not much which surprises my husband so that he is lost for words. But I arrived to find Alain utterly speechless, sitting on a straw bale, looking mesmerised at the screen where Patrick's expert testimony could be read. Patrick's statement follows.

~ * ~ * ~ * ~

The expert report of Patrick White report:

In the East Moorlands County Court   No ES 23 597

Between

Geraldine Gogarty	First Claimant
Daniel Duntz	Second Claimant
Klene Virement	Third Claimant

      And

James Enoch Birkshaw   Defendant

Expert Report

I Patrick White of Babblesprunge Farm Cobblemarkham East Moorlands do say as follows:

1. I am an expert on pig behaviour having lived all my life with pigs. I have further studied all the relevant material online from the British Pig Association, been through back copies of 'Practical Pigs' magazine and had access to 'Raising Pigs' by Lee Faber. I am aware of the views of the RSPCA https://www.rspcaassured.org.uk/farm-animal-welfare/pigs/ .I have read Practice Direction 35 of the Civil Procedure Rules. I am aware of my duties as an expert witness.

2. I understand the Claimants are instructing Dr Clive Mettange. I have not seen his report or had an opportunity to speak to him. I have read the following documents in the case:
    a. Particulars of Claim
    b. Defence and Counterclaim
    c. Defence to Counterclaim
    d. Witness statement of Geraldine Gogarty
    e. Witness statement of Daniel Duntz
    f. Witness statement of Klene Virenment
    g. Witness statement of James Enoch Birkshaw
    h. Witness statement of Gregory Bodder
    i. Witness statement of Antony Richard Robinson
    j. Witness statement of Dr William Bobbins (Fellow of the Royal Veterinary College)
    k. Scale plan of the layout of the Defendant's farm
    l. Letter of instruction

3. I have carefully read the letter of instruction and note that I have been asked specific questions about porcine behaviour which I will set out here. Essentially those questions are (i)were the

conditions in which the defendant kept his pigs cruel? (ii) did such conditions lead to the claimants being attacked? and (iii) would the behaviour have differed in the wild?

4. I understand I am not asked to comment about issues relating to the first Claimant since he never made it to the barn where the sows and piglets were being housed.

5. Pigs have been domesticated for thousands of years. It is suggested in encyclopaedias that the domestic pig is descended from the wild boar. Pigs have 44 teeth and can live for about 27 years. Pigs in the wild are gregarious and like to huddle together and maintain physical contacts. Pigs typically live in groups of about 8–10 adult sows, some youngsters and a handful single males. Pigs are omnivores who will eat anything.

6. Sows like to make a cosy nest to have their piglets. The RSPCA says:

"Around 60 per cent of female pigs (sows) are kept in farrowing crates for up to five weeks, around the time they give birth (known as 'farrowing' in pigs). While farrowing crates may help prevent the sows from lying on their piglets, they also severely restrict their movement, stopping them from being able to turn or carry out natural nesting behaviour. This can cause the animals significant stress and frustration.

What the RSPCA standards say...

The RSPCA standards strictly prohibit the use of farrowing crates. Instead, they require farrowing sows to be provided with a warm, comfortable environment with plenty of straw to help cushion and protect their piglets, whilst also allowing greater freedom of movement and the ability to express natural nesting behaviours."

7. I was born and brought up on the defendant's farm, so I am well aware of the conditions there. That is in addition to my expert knowledge of what suits pigs. As adults the defendant allows the pigs at his property to live outdoors and root around. Collections of pigs have paddocks with pig arks for shelter. There is plenty of room for rooting and wallowing. Straw is provided for bedding in the arks. Sows who are in pig have a large barn area in which to live. The floors are not slatted or bare concrete (something not approved by the RSPCA) but covered in thick straw. The sows are divided into groups and placed in a section of the barn with each area being the size of a small paddock. There is always a generous amount of straw and sometimes hay to hand and plenty of water. A feeding system ensures a continuous supply of food to the barn. I am not aware of any overcrowding. Sows are able to root in the hay and straw and the piglets are able to run around.

8. In my professional opinion the condition in which the defendant kept his pigs was not cruel. He kept his sows to the standard required by the RSCPA. In the wild, wild boars and feral pigs have to survive whatever the weather throws at them, be it drought or floods. They are prey to predators, such predators often being mankind.

9. I understand that two of the claimants attempted to remove piglets from their mothers. They were bitten and it is alleged another sow took fright and aborted her piglets. Pigs were prey animals in the wild and still can be, and 'fight or flight' can apply to their actions. No animal likes having its young picked up and removed. On the most objective level I can see no reason why the defendant should be liable for the claimants' injuries. I consider they were the authors of their own misfortune, and further caused fright to the sow who aborted her young. In the wild had the claimants

behaved in a similar manner they might have been killed and eaten. Their behaviour showed a complete lack of understanding of pig behaviour.

10. I would emphasize that although I am personally acquainted with the Defendant's property, I have written this report objectively. I literally have a lifetime's experience of porcine matters and have drawn on this and the matters I have read to arrive at my conclusions. Subjectively the claimants deserved everything that happened to them.

I confirm that I have made clear which facts and matters referred to in this report are within my own knowledge and which are not. Those that are within my own knowledge I confirm to be true. The opinions I have expressed represent my true and complete professional opinions on the matters to which they refer.'

Signed (P. White) electronic signature

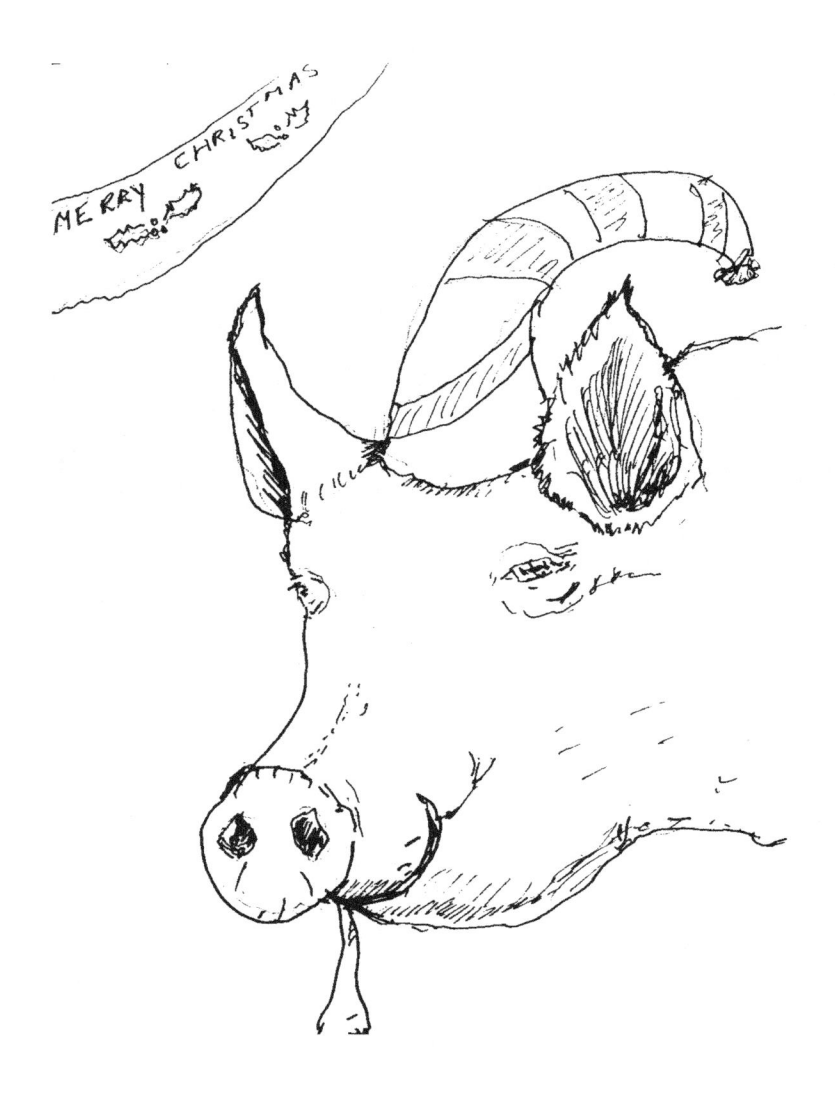

Chapter 8

Humans have strange ideas.

I thought Emmie would be pleased when I showed Alain my statement and I thought I would get more reaction from him. I thought he would see how clever I was. All he said to me was, *"I think I'll have another Scotch."*

"Could I, oink, not join you?" I queried.

It was very late, but Alain and Emmie seemed to have an argument.

"What on earth possessed you to put forward a pig as an expert witness?" said Alain.

"Jim wanted it. He said who could be more expert on pigs than a pig," said Emmie.

"The judge may well strike the evidence out," said Alain. *"In the unlikely event that does not happen the practical difficulty of producing Patrick at court would be enormous. Many will treat it as a giant publicity stunt."*

"I think in some ways Jim wants people to see Patrick, but in other ways I think he hopes the whole case would go away," said Emmie.

"Well if Patrick had to go to court he would end up being

famous. I am not sure if this is what he wants or Jim wants," said Alain.

"I think Jim wants to highlight the plight of farmers," said Emmie.

"Oink... snort. I only want to help," I said.

In the event they calmed down with regard to Jim's case Emmie soon became busy with something she called a listing questionnaire. This appeared something the court needed to finalise the trial arrangements for Jim's case. It was unclear if I would have to go to this place called 'court'. I was a little concerned about leaving my abode. It was very comfortable.

Rebecca came to chat with me one day. She brought her flask of coffee and a folding chair. She brought me some apples and some little fruits called blackberries. I like Rebecca.

"So, I hear you are an expert witness?" she said.

"Oink... I am certainly an expert on pigs," I replied.

"Do you think you were wise to volunteer?" she asked as I munched.

"It seemed like a good idea at the time... snort," I replied. "But I am not sure I really understand what happens at a court."

I continued, "What I have read says witnesses have to give an oath either swearing by Almighty God or affirming that what they say is true. But I am having trouble with this whole God and religion issue."

"A lot of people do," laughed Rebecca.

"What religion are you?" I asked her.

"Well, my parents were Jewish, but I don't practice any religion."

I snorted and thought for a minute about her reply and then I said,

"So you are from one of the religions that don't eat pigs but don't like them because you say we are unclean?" I snorted again. "Do you eat pork?"

Rebecca said, "Occasionally," in reply.

I continued, "Islam is similar in its view about pigs, but Hindus don't eat beef for different sorts of religious reasons. It's very confusing."

Rebecca said, "I wouldn't disagree."

I went on, "There is Jehovah, Allah and God and I think they are all supposed to be the same. Sikhs have one God. Christians also believe in someone called Jesus, but there are lots of different sorts of Christians. Hindus have more than one God."

Rebecca just nodded.

"Most religions have a religious book or books but mainly they are about what people believe... oink." Rebecca seemed to be listening to me.

"I am not sure what I believe or am supposed to believe," I said, "so I think I'll affirm if I have to give evidence."

Rebecca smiled at me and said, "I think I would probably affirm if I was in your position."

I continued to muse about these issues.

"It seems quite often people from one religion don't like people from another religion and often humans have wars and fights which they justify with their religion, but... oink," I added, "I think they just want an excuse to be nasty."

Rebecca nodded and I continued, "I don't need religion as an excuse to be... oink, nasty. If someone seems to be aggressive to me, I will just bite them... and as for these rules about not eating pig, I can tell you that in extreme circumstances I would eat human."

Rebecca to her credit did not look unduly perturbed. With a laugh she said,

"Would you eat me?"

"If Emmie went away and Scuffy didn't come and feed me and you fell down dead from say an accident, I can't see why I wouldn't eat you." It all seemed logical to me. "I might kill and eat someone who tried to say attack you... or Emmie... or her children...

"Changing the subject slightly... oink..." I said, "I find it difficult to understand the difference between physicists and priests..."

"How do you mean?" asked Rebecca.

"Oink. Well they both have theories they believe in about man's existence and say this is the answer..." I said. "I have watched a number of films and television programmes about how the universe came to be and some programmes about outer space. The scientists for example produce some sums to show the universe is expanding and that it all started with a 'Big Bang' but I don't think they can really explain what came before a big bang."

"It's all too clever for me," said Rebecca. "I would advise you not to get too involved in religion or how the universe came about... it's the stuff of headaches."

"Maybe," I said. "I find the study of human beings quite fascinating."

I grunted and thought for a moment and said, "I don't really understand outer space either... it all seems so, so," I had trouble expressing my thoughts adequately, "oink... big."

Rebecca laughed.

"Then," I continued, "there is Christmas, they have started going on about it on television. Christians seem to celebrate the birth of Jesus or is it the birth... oink... of Santa Claus? I am very, very confused. Jewish people also have something called Chanukah around the same time don't they... oink?"

Rebecca said, "There are a lot of religious festivals in winter. Chanukah is an eight-day religious festival of lights. Christians celebrate the birth of Jesus who they say is the Messiah come to save mankind. Santa Claus or Father Christmas was a later add-on."

I snorted. It seemed mankind needed a lot of saving and who was going to save pig-kind? Whilst I did not regret not being turned into sausages like some of my relatives and other pigs I had seen being taken away for slaughter by Emmie and Scuffy, and I also enjoyed my comforts, in some ways I regretted the knowledge I had acquired. It seemed the more one learned the more questions there were to ask. It also appeared that, as thus far, I was the only pig who could speak that had inherent dangers as well.

"Thank you, Rebecca, oink," I said, "you are very patient with my questions. I think I will concentrate on apples for now."

I stopped asking questions about religion, but then I became increasingly bothered by advertisements on television for Christmas food. It all looked so delicious. When Emmie came to see me, I asked,

"Emmie, why can't I eat human food?"

"Simple answer," she said, "it's against the law to feed farm animals with meat and animal products, or table scraps or catering waste."

"Why?" I snorted. "I mean these days I am not really a farm animal."

Emmie laughed, "Yes, you are, Patrick… you live in a barn at a farm."

"Can't I move into your house now? I am very cultured. I would go outside to do my business… people do keep pigs as pets." *I suspected I would get a negative response.*

"No," said Emmie, "you can't. You are a very large breeding boar. I think you would find it too confined. You are not some micro pig. Alain would be furious, and I suspect when it came to it you wouldn't like it."

"Why is it against the law for pigs to eat meat and meat products… snort…?" I asked.

Emmie answered, "In 2001 there was an outbreak of a terrible animal disease called Foot and Mouth disease. It might have started with some catering waste with meat from abroad. The rules are to protect animals and farmers."

I felt rather sad about the whole situation. All those advertisements for cake! How I wished I could have some. There were furniture adverts too. I had plenty of straw and hay and my own big bath, but I did like the look of human beds and settees. How I wished I could have a room in Emmie's house with my own bed and perhaps a settee or two. I mused about how nice it would be to join them at mealtimes. But I knew it was not to be. My problem was I knew much more about the world of humans than other pigs. I realised that it really would not work for me to be in Emmie's house. It would have been much better if I was a less knowledgeable pig.

The weather began to get colder. Emmie was very busy with her work. She would say things like, "I've got a will to prepare," or "I am helping the Parish Council register the Green." It didn't mean that much to me. Scuffy was rather less conversational, but he tried his best. When Alain was home, he would bring his drink of whisky to my quarters and chat to me about world affairs. Humans were forever having wars. They were also worried about something called climate change and the environment. It made sense that the air should not be nasty, and we were not so hot we burned to a crisp, although it was very pleasurable to wallow in my bath on a hot day. I didn't understand the arguments about these things. I suspected not a lot of people did, including the people who called themselves 'climate activists' or the people in charge who were called 'politicians'.

I was pleased when Charlie, Aaron and Letitia visited. Charlie would often slip a beer into me. We would put music on loudly and I would dance. I had recently become acquainted with 'War' by Edwin

Starr, and although it was not a piece of music I found particularly relaxing, it was one to which I could easily sing the words. I did a performance for Aaron and Charlie who fell about laughing. I grunted,

"I don't... oink... see the joke in this," I complained. "The song is not a cause for levity... grunt."

Charlie was getting out his phone and said, "We are laughing at your brilliance... please, please do it again."

I did another performance to the song and probably squealed "War" louder than Edwin Starr sang it. Charlie apparently filmed me, because he uploaded my performance onto social media. It became as popular as the footage of me performing 'Stayin' Alive'. I was becoming a social media phenomenon, although most people speculated the filming had been doctored. Local news media wanted to visit me again, but Emmie managed to temporarily fend them off. She said that sooner or later she would have to let them visit me again.

As we got nearer to this thing called Christmas and the weather got steadily colder, Emmie expressed concern about the lack of clarity from the court about Jim's case. Jim and Emmie discussed the matter, leaning on my barn door, peering at me.

"We have a trial window," said Emmie, "but we need a confirmed trial date. There appears to be some confusion by the court staff about the attendance of expert witnesses. Apparently, the directions for trial by the Deputy District Judge who last had hold of the court file are ambiguous. Experts to attend if possible. Video link or in person."

She continued, "I contacted the court office and indicated that a video link would be best since our expert witness to say the least, would not be able to come in an ordinary vehicle or necessarily fit in a witness box."

"I don't want to leave the farm," I said. "But if I had to make a visit somewhere not too far I suppose I would… oink… I'd need plenty of straw in my trailer and a nice bucket of fresh water…"

Emmie continued, "I spoke to a young lad on the telephone at the court. Even though the word 'pig' was mentioned I think he thought I was talking of a van for a wheelchair and a person with disabilities. I had a follow up letter indicating the 'expert's adapted van could be brought into the judges' and staff carpark'."

Jim laughed.

"You might well laugh," said Emmie, "but you complicated matters by having Patrick as an expert witness. Goodness knows how this will end!"

No more was said on the subject for a while. The humans seemed distracted by their Christmas celebrations. There were more adverts for lovely food on the television but also there was awful music described as 'Christmas music' and other slightly less bad music called Christmas carols. The latter tended to be rather serious, sometimes quite depressing tunes often sung by young boys or girls dressed in white called choristers. The awful Christmas music was performed either by younger pop singers trying to make a name for themselves or old Rockers trying to revive their careers.

The most popular Christmas offering of the year was a piece (I won't dignify it by calling it a song) performed by Polly Nea Stufe. She was apparently the next big star having wowed people at something called the Eurovision Song Contest earlier in the year. Her song called 'My growbag is my lettuce heart' had wowed the fans, and although she didn't win stardom seemed to await her. So now her Christmas song 'A tune for frozen cough sweets' was played over and over again. None of this meant anything to me except her warbling was better than the next most popular song, 'Warm mulled liquid' by an old pop-star called Sir Hill Macartford.

When Rebecca came to visit, she found me somewhat low in mood.

"Will Christmas be over soon?" I asked chewing on a swede.

"Why, don't you like it?" asked Rebecca.

"Oink... not really," I replied. "The music is terrible, and I won't get a Christmas dinner ... and I suppose I won't get presents either."

Rebecca laughed. "The music is awful. But soon Mathilda, Letitia and Aaron will be home, and I am sure they will visit you."

I cheered up a bit and said, "Maybe Aaron and his friend Charlie will bring me some beer?"

However, the principle of Christmas preyed on my mind. I wanted nice food... lots of it... and presents. It did not seem right that I would be surrounded by people who could have Christmas dinner and lots of presents and as they called it 'booze'. However, I felt concerned it would be different for me. I was sure Emmie and the family understood I could not go Christmas shopping, so my present to the family would be my amazing personality and perhaps a song. I decided to rehearse a song which I would perform if people were generous to me. The choice of song was difficult, particularly as I didn't like most of them. In the end it came down to a choice between 'Rudolf the Red-nosed Reindeer' and 'Santa Baby'. Either way I would not sing, I would sulk and just grunt a lot if people didn't give me a decent Christmas.

I need not have worried. Soon Mathilda, Letitia and Aaron came home. Charlie came to visit. Charlie and Aaron slipped beer into me. We all were having a cheerful time.

Rebecca arrived on Christmas Eve morning with two large bags. From one she decanted a metal object she called a 'pressure cooker'. Emmie was hard on her heels.

"You're mad, Mum," she said, "proposing to cook a Christmas cake for a pig."

Emmie was quite red in the face and looked rather cross.

"He is not just any pig," said Rebecca. "All the dried fruits I got from a wholesaler so no ingredients will have been near animal products. I have kind of improvised and it will give me pleasure to do. It has a carrot and potato base and dried fruits including apricots, raisins, candied peel and cherries too. It will give me pleasure to do this so let me alone…"

I watched Rebecca make her preparations; my mouth was watering. I grunted a little.

"I bought oranges and mangoes at the same warehouse," said Rebecca. "I bet you have never tasted such things… It can all be part of your Christmas dinner."

As well as Rebecca's culinary gift, Aaron and Charlie brought me a crate of beer on Christmas morning which everyone pretended not to see. Emmie brought in a large carrier bag of cooking apples on Christmas morning. Letitia came into my quarters and gave me a hug. She then tied a large woolly red and blue scarf around my neck. I would have preferred something to eat.

Mathilda and Alain came and peered at me over my door.

"Happy Christmas, pig," they said. Alain had a big carrot in his hand and Mathilda a parsnip. They tossed these somewhat token presents in my direction. I grunted. At least they had thought of me.

The humans went off to have their Christmas dinner. Scuffy was with his own family celebrating Christmas so for a while I was left to gorge myself on Rebecca's cake and mountains of fruit and vegetables.

Eventually the family sauntered outside to see me and let their dinner go down. Alain had a glass of whisky in his hand. Rebecca had a mug of coffee.

I had been snoozing. I opened my eyes slightly and grunted and then I couldn't help myself and let off an enormous fart.

"Phaw," said Alain, "there was I hoping for a song."

I awoke further and managed to get the music going.

"Santa baby," went the song, but in my case it rather came out as, "Grunty baby."

My audience seemed to enjoy the performance.

Chapter 9

(i) Good ideas can be bad ideas.

These days Jim Birkshaw had something of a bee in his bonnet about his court case which now had a date at the very end of February, and he seemed mildly obsessed about how having Patrick as his expert witness was going to highlight the plight of pig farmers and show up animal rights' protestors as extremists. I really felt the whole idea of Patrick being an expert was now going to be doomed to disaster. Either Jim and I were going to be dismissed as raving nut cases or the world's press would come and try and see Patrick. As it was, I was aware Patrick's singing and dancing was a bit of a hit on social media. I surmised crazy scientists might want to kidnap him and take him away.

I made it clear to my opponents and the court I did not see the need for experts to attend. This was supposed to be a 1-day Fast Track trial. I was content to deal with Dr Clive Mettange's lack of personal experience with pigs by submissions. My opponents did not seem that bothered if our expert attended or not. Nonetheless, the last judge looking at the case had appeared to direct experts to attend. I tried a last-minute application and sought an urgent telephone hearing. What I got was a written set of directions as follows:

"Order

Upon reading the defendant's urgent application and noting the defendant's expert needs special facilities if he is to attend court

Upon urging the experts to meet

Upon noting the Claimant's expert has expressed a lack of willingness to engage with the Defendant's expert in a telephone conference

It is ordered that:

1. The parties' solicitors shall notify the court forthwith if expert evidence has now been agreed.

2. In the event expert evidence has still not been agreed the parties' solicitors shall inform the court office within 48 hours if the evidence can now be heard by telephone.

3. In the event experts are still attending court, special arrangements shall be made for any special vehicle adapted, modified or otherwise.

4. Permission to apply on short notice to vary or set aside this order".

ALAIN FOUND ME WITH MY head in my hands.

"You look miserable and wretched," he said.

"You certainly know how to cheer a girl up," I responded. The order fell on the floor. Alain picked it up.

"Don't read it… client privilege," I said.

"Pooh," said Alain looking at the order. "You dropped it and I'm your husband." Then he said,

"Who will do the advocacy?"

"Me," I replied.

"No disrespect, Emmie," said Alain, "but you need someone who can put a bit of distance between this situation and him or herself."

"Jim can't afford good counsel... Besides, who would accept a brief for this? Cab rank rule would go out of the window," I said.

"I'll do it," said Alain. "I'll do it pro bono too... if only to stop all of you digging an even bigger hole for yourselves."

"I am sure Jim will be delighted," I responded.

"Don't think there isn't some self-interest here," Alain continued. "I don't want my reputation sullied by your misadventures with a talking and dancing pig. I also think the whole family would be upset if Patrick was carted off and dissected... you seem to have grown somewhat attached to him, which is something you said you would never do with a farm animal. I think he gets more attention these days than Piecrust."

He patted our family dog on the head as he had appeared on hearing his name.

Jim Birkshaw was delighted that Alain would be counsel at the trial. Although Alain had said he would act 'pro bono' he insisted on paying a small fee to cover Alain's travel expenses plus a nominal amount on the top.

"And," said Jim, "if I win I will buy him a good bottle of Scotch... twenty-year-old single malt."

Alain went through the documents with a fine-tooth comb. He made some discreet inquiries via his clerk as to who would be instructed for the claimants. I think he nurtured hopes of having some discussions with counsel for the claimants to try to gain agreement that experts should not attend the trial. Unfortunately, counsel for the claimant was Miss Beverley St-Paul Artemis a strident lady well known for representing lost causes. Despite Alain's best efforts, discussions did not take place.

I wondered if last minute intervention by the trial judge might be achieved. It seemed that was not to be either. When I had learned of the actual trial date, I had wrongly assumed the local District Judge would hear the case. However, it appeared the lead Civil Circuit Judge for the district was visiting the court unexpectedly for that week, and the listing officer wanted to occupy him. Thus, the trial was to come before His Honour Judge Winston Armstrong KC. Something of a rising star amongst the judiciary, he was the son of 'Windrush' immigrants, and had climbed up the greasy pole by his sheer determination and intelligence. He and his husband, a well-known cardiologist had also adopted disabled twins, wounded in conflicts in the Horn of Africa. He had also written the pre-eminent thesis on good governance in LGBT organisations and an easy-to-read book on how litigants in person could navigate the courts without lawyers. He had a reputation for his wit and compassion but also, he did not suffer fools gladly.

I sent a last-minute message to the court to ask whether His Honour really wanted Mr White at court… surely a video link would do? I was told in a telephone call by the judge's clerk, "His Honour is looking forward to meeting Mr White in person."

"Oh dear," said Alain, "not what we wanted."

Thus, I had to make arrangements with Scuffy to take Patrick in a trailer to the court. Jim Birkshaw's man Greg agreed to accompany Scuffy. He was a witness so needed to be present at the trial in any event. I agonised as to whether I needed to go online and complete a pig-movement licence which would be the normal and legal thing to do before transporting one of my pigs. In the end I gave up. Patrick was not going to another farm or an abattoir or a sale or an agricultural show. I just hoped I was not breaking a load of rules.

I would be travelling with Alain rather than with the trailer, so I made it my business to have a good talk with Patrick to try and explain where he was going, and that he would return to his own quarters. We looked at pictures of court rooms online. I tried to find films of courtroom dramas, but many of the films or tv shows were American. They were also mainly dramas about criminal proceedings. I hoped I had not given Patrick the wrong impression.

(ii) *Humans have odd ideas*

I was to be an expert witness in Jim's court case. I was excited and scared by the prospect. I was excited about seeing something of the human world, and apprehensive about leaving the safety of Emmie's farm. She had shown me television programmes with courtroom scenes. A lot of them were about humans called Americans who spoke English like Emmie and I except it had some different words which made it rather confusing for me. Sweets were called 'candies' and taps were called 'faucets', for example. In television programmes Americans seemed to have really big cars which they drove at high speed and put something called 'gas' in them. There seemed to be a lot of shooting. Emmie said this was not necessarily true to life.

Most of the American television dramas with court scenes were about murders, which did not surprise me since there was so much shooting. Humans took the killing of other humans very seriously. There appeared to be both an important person called a judge who knew how courts worked and twelve ordinary people called a jury, who didn't know how things worked, to decide if somebody did it or not. It seemed a bit over the top to me. The American lawyers (people who did the same job as Emmie and Alain) seemed rather dramatic people who would loudly say things like "objection Your Honour" or "sidebar Your Honour". Emmie said things were a bit less loud in English courts and as this was a civil case there would only be a Judge to decide the outcome.

Emmie said she hoped I would never set foot in the courtroom, and that people would see sense. More to the point I could not see how I would fit in parts of a courtroom. I certainly could not see how I would fit in a witness box. She agreed with me over that point.

Scuffy and Flemmy gave me something of a scrubbing before I was loaded into the trailer. They said humans would prefer it if I was all pink and clean. The trailer itself was designed to take about six pigs so I would have plenty of room.

Scuffy was using his strong 4-wheel drive to pull it and Greg would sit up front with him, rather than riding in my trailer. Jim was travelling from his farm and Emmie and Alain set out together really early to be well on time. We were quite early too. We needed to get there for ten o'clock in human time which in my time was 'mid-morning snack time'.

As we travelled down the farm track to the road, I remembered my arrival at Emmie's farm. It all seemed such a long time ago.

We bumped and rattled along. I could see glimpses of the outside world through tiny, slatted windows. I didn't risk standing on my hindlegs to gaze over the backdoors at the outside world as I seemed to sway around. In some areas there were large numbers of humans' houses. Eventually we seemed to come to a stop, and I hoped we had arrived. However, Scuffy tapped the side of my trailer and shouted,

"Just stopping for fuel and sarnies, won't be long."

First, I peered out of the little slatted windows at the sides. I could see quite a few other vehicles. The place had a funny smell. People were putting hoses of something into the backs of their cars and trucks. They were going backwards and forwards to a building. Some people came out with what looked to be food in their hands. After a few minutes I suppose I became impatient. I went to the back of the trailer where there was a larger opening. With a tremendous effort I raised myself onto my back legs and rested my front trotters on top of the door, poking my head out. I couldn't see Scuffy and Greg. A woman with a somewhat small girl who I assumed was her piglet walked past. The child pointed to me and said,

"Look, Mummy, there's a funny piggy."

I still could not see Scuffy and Greg and I was getting a bit anxious. The sight of the humans with food and drink was also making me hungry and thirsty so I called out,

"Hello, oink, hello, where are you?"

There was no reply, but I heard the small child say, "Mummy, Mummy the piggy is speaking."

Foolishly, not thinking of the consequences, I replied, "Hello... oink... have you seen my people?"

A few people's heads turned. The mother of the child seemed to drop one of those hose things and black stuff came squirting out. She also screamed and shouted,

"There's a talking pig."

People began to stare at me. I saw another person drop their hose thing and more black stuff squirting out.

Greg suddenly appeared, closely followed by Scuffy.

"Shhhh," they both called out.

I responded, "I am... oink... oink... hungry."

"I've got some apples and turnips in the truck," said Scuffy, but not before the little girl pulled away from her mother and came to the back of my trailer.

"I'm Molly," she said. "What's your name?" she asked.

It would have been rude not to reply so I said, "Oink... Patrick."

She handed me a bar of something which smelled absolutely delicious. I knew from previous contact with humans not to eat her fingers or they would be cross. Therefore, I took it carefully.

"You can have my chocolate," she said. "Mummy said I eat too many sweets anyway."

It was wonderful. I grunted a big "thank you". By then Scuffy was trying to offer me water from a plastic bucket into which he poured water from a bottle together with a big apple. A crowd of curious people looked at me. There were murmurings about "talking pig" and "is that the dancing pig from the internet?". A few took my picture. Some called out at me things like, "Hello, piggy piggy."

Then a white car with blue and yellow markings and the word 'Police' appeared. Greg hissed to Scuffy, "Best scarper."

Scuffy called to me, "Get down, get down... we are going," as he ran to get back in his vehicle. Greg called out, "Show's over, folks," from the passenger window.

I had already climbed down and as we moved away, I could see a man in a dark blue uniform get out of the police car.

We had not gone very far when I was aware of the police car approaching us. It had its lights on and 'nee-nee' noises seem to come from it. We came to a stop. I wondered if we had done something wrong because I recalled from watching television that there were often chases on American roads called freeways. Police or as they called them 'Cops' would noisily chase bad men. As we came to a stop, I could hear both Greg and Scuffy getting out of the car. Scuffy ran around to me while Greg was talking to two policemen.

Scuffy hissed at me, "'ave you forgotten everything our Emmie said about not attracting attention? Now act stupid like you can't talk properly... like you did for the reporter."

I was getting rather worried. I realised maybe I should have kept quiet when we had stopped. I did not want to get arrested. Greg and the policemen walked around to me. They were chatting. Greg was saying,

"Yes, he is the pig that did the little dance on social media... but I think people were getting a bit carried away at the petrol station."

"Are you on the way to an agricultural show?" asked one police officer.

"Something like that," Greg replied.

Scuffy chipped in, "Do you want to see our drivers' licenses? We have nothing to hide... just farm people transporting a pig."

One of the policemen said, "Can you get him to say 'hello'?"

Scuffy said, "Say 'hello' to the nice policeman."

I said an "oink-oink" which vaguely sounded like "hello". I was not at all sure the policeman was nice, and I was sure Scuffy was just speaking like this to humour him.

"Can you join in a bit of 'Old Macdonald'?" said Scuffy glaring at me.

Greg and Scuffy started a poor rendition of the song, and I made noises at the relevant places. Our performance was pretty bad, and after a few minutes the policemen were covering their ears.

"Okay, okay, that's enough," said one of them. "I think the people at the petrol station were getting hysterical over nothing. He's just a pig... we've got better things to do but thank you for the performance."

They turned and returned to their police car and after giving us a friendly wave drove off.

Scuffy spoke to me, "While we finish the journey please keep a low profile. Also, when we first get to the court wait for our Emmie to tell you what to do... you could 'ave got Greg and I into a load of bother, not to mention what might 'ave 'appened to you."

"Yes," said Greg, "I think we have all had a lucky escape."

They gave me some more water in a bucket before we continued the journey.

I could see more houses and buildings with brightly coloured signs which I understood were shops. I also saw many cars and lorries. They made a kind of nasty oily smell like an old tractor. Now and again, we stopped briefly surrounded by other vehicles. At last, we seemed to come off the busy roads and we seemed to stop at the entrance to something. I could see through the slats that there was a gateway with a little narrow shed. A man came out of the little shed and spoke to Scuffy and Greg.

Greg said,

"We've brought the expert witness for the trial."

The man said,

"I was told there would be a special vehicle... I didn't think it would be an animal trailer."

Scuffy said, "Well it's what Patrick travels in..."

"Okay," said the man, "you best park it over in that far corner of the carpark. Shall I call a member of staff to help Mr White into the building?"

"No," said Scuffy. "Can they just notify either Mr or Mrs Martyns he is here? He will wait in the trailer for now."

The man looked surprised but agreed this is what he would do. He went back into the shed, and we pulled into a far area of the carpark.

Scuffy came round to check I was alright and to remind me to maintain a low profile for the time being.

"Oink, oink... What happens next?" I asked as quietly as I could.

Scuffy shrugged and replied, "I've no bloody idea."

Chapter 10

The trial

East Moorlands Combined Court had become my 'local' court after the court in the neighbouring town closed in the name of progress. The local court had the advantage for litigants that they did not have to travel for miles on poor transport (note I did not say public). The staff, magistrates and judges knew the local landscape. Be that as it may, Alain and I were stuck with Jim's case being in East Moorland Combined Court and so we set off there on a fine crisp day at the end of February.

The court building had been constructed in the nineteen seventies and the front was sandwiched between East Moorlands Town Hall and East Moorlands Minster (otherwise known as St Rita's Minster), a fine Gothic style church of considerable age. A somewhat insalubrious pub (which in its heyday had been a coaching inn and seat of the assize court) had apparently been pulled down to create space for the court which went back some distance onto the ground of what had apparently once been an abattoir. The staff carpark had once been a small cattle market and the holding pens for the animals going to the abattoir. I shivered with nerves at the irony of Patrick going there.

"Are you okay, Em?" said Alain as we pulled into a multi-storey carpark. I nodded and continued to think about the court. I thought again about Patrick being brought to the site of the old abattoir and I hoped that it would not worry him if he found out.

At the rear of the court the staff carpark was bounded by a walled carpark for the Town Hall staff on one side, but on the other side was a sizeable cemetery and the rear entrance to the Minster. There was a tall dry-stone wall which marked the boundary between the court carpark and the cemetery which must have been particularly welcome when the abattoir and cattle market was operational. The road behind the court and the Minster was a 'no through road' since the space behind the town hall also had some overflow offices and the Moorlands River known colloquially as 'Rita's Ditch' ran alongside the other side of the road and the overflow council offices. It eventually emptied into a big lake.

Inside the court building the ground floor housed the court offices plus a room with windows for the public and lawyers to speak to court staff, the main public toilets, a Citizens' Advice Bureau office, a coffee stall run by volunteers, a couple of rooms for advocates to meet clients and a bank of lifts. On the first floor, courts one and two could be found with a waiting hall as well as a barristers' changing room, a solicitors' room, more toilets and another advocates' meeting room. On the second floor was the slightly smaller court three, two district judges' chambers, another two advocates' meeting room, a waiting area, and a disabled toilet. On the third floor of the building was a slightly inconveniently situated district judge's chambers since there was no waiting area, the jury retiring area and what I believed were more offices because I obviously had no access there. I recalled that in old literature about the court there had been a canteen on the third floor but that had been closed down presumably in the same spate of closures which led to the demise of my local court.

Alain and I took a short walk from the multi-storey carpark to the front of the court. There were a couple of film cameramen near the front of the court, but they were actually more interested in St Rita's Minster, as were a handful of policemen who were milling about. It seemed an irony that we had the possibility of a pig giving evidence in a court door to a Minster church dedicated to the patron saint of the impossible. When we stopped at the security arch for court security to check our bags, I asked the security guards what was going on at the Minster.

"Well," said one of them, "some Royal is going to attend a service of dedication for the new stained glass window. I hope there won't be trouble… there is a rumour that climate activists might try and disrupt the service since the window has been sponsored by an oil rig engineering company."

I nodded my head and made sympathetic noises, even though I was relieved it had nothing to do with Patrick. The guard continued,

"I don't know why they are all at the front. They will most likely use the rear entrance of the Minster."

I shivered and thought of Patrick who I knew was due to arrive in the court carpark behind the court.

Once we got into the main foyer we checked the noticeboard for the location of the trial.

"As I thought," said Alain, "court 3. Courts 1 and 2 have access from the cells and more room for jurors so they will consign civil work to court 3."

I nodded in agreement as he continued, "I will go to the robing room and get changed. Can you by any chance go up and wait outside court 3 for our client and our witnesses?"

"Yes, of course," I said as we headed for the lifts. Alain disembarked at the first floor to go to the barristers' changing room while I continued to the first floor.

Jim was already there in the waiting area, sitting with his farmhand Tony. He looked rather pale.

"I think the claimants are here already," he said, gesticulating to the other side of the room. Two men and a woman were sitting on a bench. A tall fully robed female barrister resplendent in her wig and gown was pacing up and down in front of them. She appeared to spot me speaking to Jim and approached with a long stride.

"You," she said to me, "yes, you. Are you appearing for Mr Birkshaw today?"

"I am Mrs Martyns, the instructing solicitor," I replied.

"Well who is counsel… I don't want to speak to you," said the woman who I assumed was Miss Beverley St. Paul Artemis.

Through gritted teeth I replied, "Mr Alain Martyns."

"Oooh the husband," she responded and began to laugh sounding something akin to a donkey crossed with a screech-owl, if that were possible. Fortunately, Alain appeared quickly.

"I want a word," she hee-hawed after I introduced him.

"Well, I just need to report to the usher," smiled Alain.

He went to the usher at the entrance to court 3 who was a pleasant, smiling, middle-aged lady with badge indicating she was called 'Nicky Nichols'.

"Ah, yes," she said, "I have a message to tell you that your witness Gregory Bodder is on his way into the building and your expert Mr White is in his vehicle in the carpark."

"Thank you," said Alain, "I am hoping we may not need the expert."

"Oh," said the usher, "His Honour said he was particularly looking forward to meeting him."

I felt a shiver again.

In the event, after what seemed to be an age, we took our places in court 3. I sat with Jim behind Alain. Further along the long, green leather bench sat the three claimants and a very young-looking girl who appeared to be their solicitors' representative. The judge's clerk (who I understand was called Tom Cooper) announced,

"Gogarty, Duntz, and Virenment versus Birkshaw, case number E S 23597, all rise please."

His Honour Judge Winston Armstrong KC entered the court and started to sit down behind the judicial table.

"Sit, please," he said but Miss St. Paul Artemis did not sit down and said loudly,

"I have an application, Your Honour."

His Honour's handsome visage broke into a faint smile. "Already? We haven't started yet. Sit down until I say otherwise."

He made himself comfortable and carefully arranged his papers. He put his pens in a neat row. It was as if he was making her wait. Then he looked up,

"Now," he said, "be so kind as to make the introductions of who is in my court and then tell me what application you wish to make."

She haughtily explained who everyone was and then said,

"Now, Your Honour, I wish to apply to have the defendant's expert evidence on pig behaviour struck out."

"Why?" said His Honour smiling even more.

"Because of his lack of formal qualifications and because he is not here," she replied.

"Well my clerk tells me that he is here... in the carpark," said His Honour. "Is your expert here?"

She replied that he was not.

"Is that a problem, Mr Martyns?" His Honour asked Alain who

answered, "Not a problem. I understand Dr Clive Mettange is an anthropologist who admits he has never set foot on a pig farm, so I am content to make submissions about his evidence at the appropriate time, Your Honour."

"There we are then," said His Honour with a chuckle, "I understand medical evidence is agreed. I hope the other witnesses won't take too long. Then I shall hear Mr White."

Miss St. Paul Artemis looked crestfallen.

"Shall I open for the claimants now, Your Honour?" she queried.

"Yes," said His Honour, "but unless you have anything seismic to add for Mr Gogarty I can give you the clearest indication now that people who drive into ditches in order to trespass are not going to get very far… well except to have mishaps."

She looked even more crestfallen. "But, Your Honour, it was a very deep ditch," she stammered.

"Many ditches are," said His Honour. "Get on with it."

The disappointed barrister for the claimants rattled and stammered through her opening to their case. Alain made a very brief opening for Jim.

The claimants were called in turn to give evidence. Alain had grasped the lie of the land, so he kept his cross-examination succinct. To Mr Gogarty he asked,

"When you drove into the ditch was there any roadway, track, drive or path where you were attempting to drive?"

The answer was of course in the negative.

The other two witnesses gave evidence as expected. Alain briefly cross-examined each of the witnesses questioning each of them as to whether they were aware of RSPCA standards and whether they understood that their own behaviour distressed the sows and led to their injuries. Each witness gave answers as expected that they considered it unfair for there to be captive farm animals and that such animals needed to be freed. I thought I heard the judge make a little 'guffaw'.

Miss St. Paul Artemis then made reference to Dr Mettange's report.

Alain said, "If it pleases, Your Honour, the defendant does not accept a report from an anthropologist who has never visited a pig farm has any weight in this case. I will make more detailed submissions in closing arguments."

His Honour Judge Armstrong just nodded, smiling broadly.

It was now time for Alain to call Jim and then Tony and Greg. Alain dealt with evidence in chief briefly. The cross-examination from Miss St. Paul Artemis was as expected. Jim and his employees were challenged about the conditions of his pigs, and indeed about the principles of keeping farm animals. They all held up very well. Alain kept everything low-key and to his credit that showed off the weaknesses in the claimants' case.

After a very brief lunch break, we reconvened.

"And now," said His Honour Judge Armstrong with a smile on his face, "it is time to hear from Mr White."

"Shall I send the usher to fetch him upstairs, Your Honour?" asked the clerk, Mr Cooper.

I sat there with a cold sweat wondering how on earth Patrick could be brought up to court 3 let alone fit in the witness box. But His Honour Judge Winston Armstrong KC said,

"No, of course not. We are going to him. Please make sure we have the portable recording equipment. We are reconvening in the carpark in five minutes by Mr White's vehicle."

Everyone piled into the lifts and security showed us through to the staff carpark. His Honour Judge Winston Armstrong KC, Nicky and Tom Cooper had arrived just ahead of us, presumably using a staff lift.

They were standing at the rear of the trailer. I wondered what was going to happen next.

His Honour said,

"Can I meet Mr White now?"

I called out, "Patrick show yourself... time to give evidence," and once again felt a shiver of nerves.

There was a snorting, and a snuffling noise and Patrick drew himself up on his hind legs and looked out of the rear of the trailer with his trotters resting on the door.

"It's a pig," screamed Miss St Paul Artemis.

"I know," said His Honour smiling. "Don't you watch social media? Didn't you see Patrick White the dancing pig?"

Mr Cooper spoke. "Why have we got the recording equipment, Your Honour? Surely a pig can't give evidence?"

"Oh yes. Oink... I can," said Patrick. "I wish... oink... to be heard."

"It's a trick, a trick," screamed Miss St Paul Artemis.

"If you are alleging trickery," said the judge, "you should say 'It's a trick, Your Honour'. As it is I think we should open the back doors of the trailer to make sure no-one else is in there and to make the pig more comfortable."

"Would that be safe?" queried Mr Cooper.

"Would it be safe?" echoed His Honour, looking at Alain and I.

Alain replied, "Your Honour, it would be perfectly safe. Patrick White is an exceptional pig as you will find out."

"There we are then," said His Honour with a smile.

The back of the trailer was opened so Patrick did not have to stand on his rear quarters.

"I hope the portable recording equipment is on," said His Honour. Nicky confirmed that it was.

Mr Cooper asked, "Do you wish the animal sworn?"

Patrick called out, "I am not just 'the animal'... I am Patrick White. I don't like swearing and bad language. Oink."

"That is not necessary," said His Honour Judge Armstrong KC. "If no-one objects I will just ask Patrick White a few questions myself?"

Alain indicated he had no objections and Miss St. Paul Artemis just made a sort of gulping noise.

"First," said His Honour, "do you know who I am?"

"You are the judge," said Patrick. "I thought... oink... you would know that. That is why you are wearing that funny outfit. Oink."

"Now," said His Honour to Patrick, "do you know the difference between the truth and a lie?"

"Oink... of course," said Patrick. "A lie would be to say this was a nice place... the truth would be to say I would rather be at the farm."

His Honour continued, "Could you continue to tell the truth for me?"

"Yes... oink... of course."

"Are you able to tell me how you are able to speak?" questioned His Honour.

"I don't altogether know... oink," said Patrick who continued to give a potted history of himself.

"During that time you are saying you have learned to read and with speech recognition equipment to write?" queried the judge, who was smiling all the time.

"Oink, yes indeed... I have read lots of things," said Patrick. "Rules to do with courts, RSPCA standards... trashy novels most recently..."

"And writing?"

"Yes, with speech equipment... Did you know I even did a statement for this case?" queried Patrick.

"Yes, I was going to ask you about it... Did you really do it all yourself or did someone help you?"

Patrick made a loud snort. "Well, of course Charlie and Aaron had to set up all the equipment... I am a pig... I couldn't do that. The words are all mine. It's all correct. Those men should not have gone near those sows."

"Who are Charlie and Aaron?" asked His Honour.

"Human friends... Aaron is studying... oink... sports... and Charlie is his friend... oink... good with equipment but I think otherwise a silly boy."

"Is there anything else you want to add?" queried the judge.

"Yes," said Patrick. "I don't like it here. Oink... please can I go home now... or even to Jim's farm?"

His Honour Judge Winston Armstrong KC said,

"It's been a pleasure to meet you. I think you should be allowed to go home as soon as possible," then he turned to Alain and Miss St Paul Artemis, "any objections?"

They shook their heads. Miss St Paul Artemis was very pale.

"Mr White and the lay witnesses are released," said His Honour. "I would like to see the advocates and their solicitors in my chambers in ten minutes."

We went back into the court building after I had given the nod to Scuffy and Greg to take Patrick home. Something seemed to be going on at the back of the Minster, but it didn't occur to me it would affect Patrick.

After a few minutes we found ourselves in the judge's chambers.

"You may all sit down," he said. After a pause he continued,

"I think a little damage limitation is needed by everyone," he said.

"Your Honour," started Beverley St. Paul Artemis, "I must protest about that pig..."

"Oh do be quiet and hear me out," said His Honour, sounding annoyed. "Let's look at the picture. First, I own up to having kids in my household who show me stuff on social media, and I am interested in the countryside including farm animals! I was already aware there was this pig called Patrick White who joined in 'Old Macdonald'…and danced. Then I read the expert reports… then my clerk told me about the 'expert' coming in a special vehicle… I fully expected a pig to arrive, and I am amazed the claimants didn't spot this."

He paused and leaned back in his chair.

"What really surprised me this afternoon is the level of his speech and understanding…"

"But, Your Honour," Miss St. Paul Artemis started again.

"Oh please stop interrupting… it will not do you any favours not to hear me out," the judge continued.

"Now, I see it like this. I suppose the claimants could object to the pig's evidence and call for his examination by veterinary surgeons. And tests about his ability to speak. But would that not be counter-productive to their arguments that they are all about animal welfare? The defence will no doubt argue with some strength that I should give no weight to Dr Clive Mettange's report. As it is I will take a lot of persuading that the first claimant's case has anything in it at all… he seems to have driven himself in a ditch.

"The defendant needs to give thought to what happens if I give a reasoned judgment giving weight to the presence of this remarkable animal at court. Do he and for that matter the pig want the publicity it could attract…? It is one thing to have a pig brought to the court carpark, but quite another for there to be a judgment which could be downloaded and published.

"Now, I can't force the parties to settle but I want to give you half an hour to see if that is what you want."

He smiled. He then allowed us to withdraw. Miss St. Paul Artemis was an even funnier colour. Some negotiations took place. The claimants agreed to drop their claims in return for Jim dropping his counterclaim. They grudgingly agreed to pay 75% of Jim's costs at fixed fast track rates with the exception of any costs relating to expert evidence! A draft consent order was drawn up for the judge's approval.

Jim was delighted with the outcome (as was I). The claimants and their counsel looked rather miserable as they left the court. As Alain and I were leaving we could hear quite a lot of noise from the area of the Minster. As we passed the security men who had checked us in we exchanged cheerful banter. They told us some 'Just Block Oil' activists were protesting behind St Rita's Minster because of the sponsorship of the stained glass window by the oil rig engineering company.

"Well I am glad I am going home," I said, "I have seen enough drama for one day."

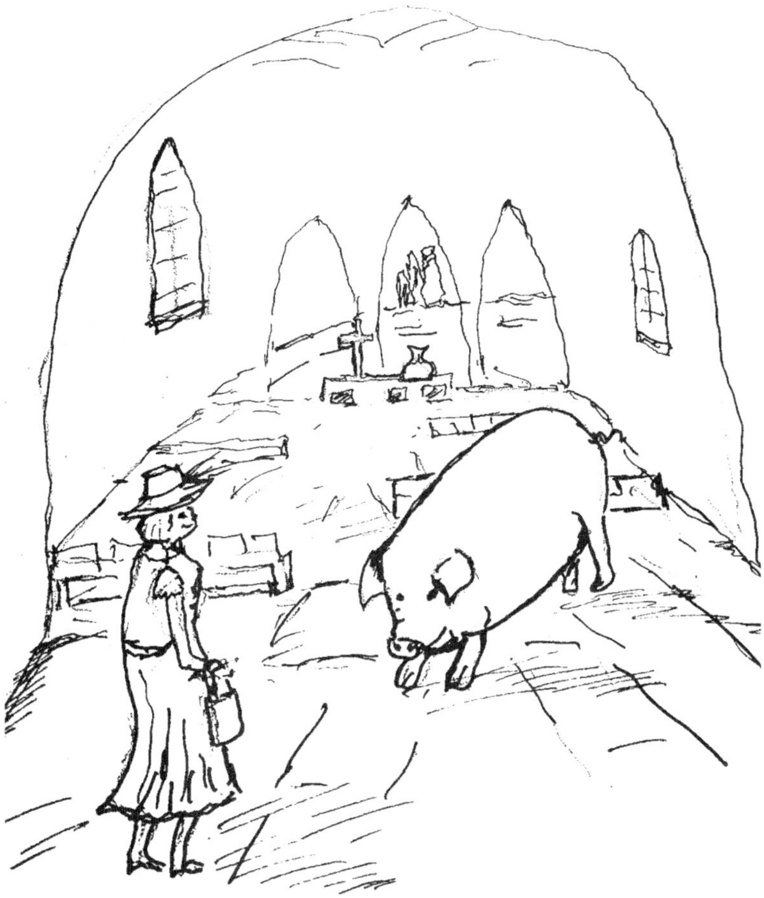

Chapter 11

(i) Oil and Royal

*T*here are so many things which don't make sense about humans. For example, there is a king and queen who are the top people, sort of in charge, but not in charge. Then there are politicians who people can choose to have in charge of them. Every few years they get to choose these political leaders at a time called an election and after that they are supposed to be in charge. The king and queen have relatives called the Royal Family or 'Royals' who are important, but it is politicians who have a thing called the government who are supposed to run things and sort things out.

Sometimes people not in the government don't like something. They get together and make a noise about it. I think I understand that. Sometimes I make a noise if I disagree with something. But sometimes people do worse things than just making a noise. It seemed these 'Just Block Oil' people did things like glue themselves to roads which seemed very uncomfortable. I can't say I understood their reasoning. It also made other people cross when they could not get down the road. I could not understand how being glued to somewhere helped the 'Just Block Oil' people with their argument. I don't understand why they didn't try to be politicians and try to get chosen in an election to be the government.

I know they are unhappy about climate change. Being a pig, I really don't understand the arguments either way. Also, being a pig, I don't understand whether we should stop using all oil as soon as possible or not. What I do understand is that getting in the way and blocking things up makes people very, very cross. I know if I get in the way it makes Emmie very cross. So, I think just gluing oneself to places and getting in the way is going to make people very cross, rather than seeing one's point of view. Also, it must be very uncomfortable.

As for the Royals I thought it would be rather nice to have all those big houses like they had, but they did seem to have to do a lot of annoying things like visit hospitals where I understood humans put poorly humans, and meet politicians.

When we are about to leave the court carpark there seemed to be a loud noise from behind the building next door which the humans called a Minster. There was both cheering and booing. We stopped at the gates and the security man said,

"You might have a job getting through... it seems the Royal personage is just entering the churchyard but there are 'Block Oil' protesters trying to glue themselves to the Royal limousine."

Greg replied, "Well, we have to try. We have a pig in the trailer, and he needs to be away from the town and back at the farm."

We seemed to turn out into the street. I could see through the slats there were crowds of people being held back by the police. Some were waving little flags and calling out, "God save the king and queen." Others had big banners saying, 'Block Oil' and were yelling, "Booo."

A police officer on a motorbike was speaking to Scuffy and Greg and was indicating that he would try to make a passage through for us. I could see there was a big, black, shiny car just pulling in by the churchyard.

We crawled forward just as I could see the doors opening of the limousine. Suddenly, part of the crowd moved forward and seemed to surge towards us. I could feel the trailer being rocked backwards and forwards and voices yelling, "Block oil, block oil, kill the police, kill the police, kill the pigs." I was terrified since I thought they wanted to kill me, so when the rocking caused the doors of my trailer to burst open, I jumped out and ran.

Although I could hear Greg and Scuffy calling my name by then I was in a grassy area with big stones which I understood to be the churchyard. Ahead of me a tall, nice-looking lady in a smart coat with a matching hat was being shown inside by a man in a long white robe. The police had managed to hold back the crowd from the churchyard but when they saw me there were cries of, "Pig, pig, pig." The door of the Minster was still open, so I headed towards it, using a slightly circuitous route behind the stones to try to avoid being seen.

By the time I got inside the smart lady who I later discovered was the Royal and the man in the robe who I later discovered was called a bishop, were at the other end of the building staring upwards at a coloured glass window. There were a couple of men in suits with them. They did not notice me initially. I sat down somewhat exhausted between a row of seats.

Soon I could hear some shouting near the open doorway,

"Stay back, stay back... there's a live pig in there. He could be dangerous."

Three police officers were holding people back and talking into devices I now understand are police radios. They looked like oversized mobile phones. One of the men in suits with the tall Royal lady was talking into a radio as well.

Scuffy and Greg were at the doorway arguing with the police to be let through to me. They were calling to me,

"Patrick, Patrick... come on... let's try and get back to the farm."

I hesitated as I was scared of the crowds and frankly scared of the police as well.

One of the police officers on the radio spoke to a man in a suit,

"Maybe we will have to get a marksman and shoot the animal... I don't know if he's dangerous," said the police officer.

I could hear faintly the man in the suit talking to the bishop who was saying,

"The quicker the better... I don't want a dirty, smelly pig on consecrated ground."

I shivered in fear and could hear Scuffy and Greg arguing my case,

"Don't you even think of doing that... please. He is not at all dangerous... he's Patrick White... the pig who sings and dances on social media."

Then I heard a haughty voice (from the Royal lady) say, "Give me that radio," and then she said down the radio, "you will not shoot the pig. I want to meet him. Also, you will do everything you can to help him get back to his farm after I have met him."

Then I heard her say to the bishop, "As for you, you are a disgrace to the Church. His Majesty the king likes animals... I can't imagine he would want this creature shot for no sensible reason that I can discern."

With that she strode down the aisle of the building towards me. I came out from behind the seats and did a sort of bow,

"Thank you. Thank you... Your... your... oink," I did not know what to call her, "Magnificence?"

She smiled and laughed.

"I don't know how or why you are here," she said, "but I think the best place for you is back on your farm."

"Oink, yes please," I replied and then I said, "can I... oink, sing for you... before I go...?"

"That would be absolutely splendid," replied the Royal person.

I tried to remember something. It was very difficult. I just managed a couple of lines,

"Oink save our Gracious King, long live our Oink-sious King, oink live our King."

She clapped her hands together. "That was absolutely spiffing. I can't wait to tell the king."

She called to the bishop, "They do say St Rita is the patron saint of the impossible... well I have just had a splendid chat with a pig."

Then she proceeded to calmly and loudly give out orders. First, Scuffy and Greg were to be allowed to reverse the trailer up the path through the churchyard to the Minster door. Then, after I was loaded inside the police were to give priority to escorting us up the street. The Minster door was to be closed so the Royal personage could be safe inside, listening to the service of dedication. The police were to deal with escorting her out later. It seemed that fortunately while I was in the Minster a lot of police reinforcements had arrived. They had managed to hold the crowds back and stop anyone wrecking our trailer. It had a few slogans sprayed on it 'Block Oil' and 'Kill the pigs', but fortunately it was strongly built.

One demonstrator had glued himself to the Minster railings. The police seemed to be giving him low priority and were prioritising getting us on our way, so we had a motor-cycle escort for part of our journey. I hoped the protestor who was stuck to the railings was very uncomfortable as he seemed a very silly man.

Once the motor-cycled police left us we pulled off the road and stopped in what I believe humans call a lay-by. It was beginning to get dark. Both Scuffy and Greg came and spoke to me.

"Are you OK?" they both asked.

"I was scared... those people said kill the pigs," I said.

"Reckon they meant the police," said Scuffy. "They call police 'pigs' as a kind of insult."

I did not understand that at all. Indeed, there was so much of the world I found bewildering.

Scuffy and Greg offered me some water and poured some water from some small bottles into a bucket. I think it was their own drinking water and although it was not very much, I was grateful to have it and said, "Oink, many thanks."

The rest of the journey was mercifully uneventful, and by the time we reached home it was completely dark. Emmie and Alain had got home first. They had caught something on the radio and then the television about a Royal visit at St Rita's Minster, demonstrations and a runaway pig.

"Thank goodness you are all alright," said Emmie to Scuffy, Greg and myself. Scuffy was concerned about the slogans on the trailer, but Emmie said,

"People and pig are far more important."

Even Alain seemed pleased to see me in one piece. I was really glad to be back in my quarters. Emmie made sure I had a long drink of water and gave me some pig nuts and some apples which I gobbled down since I found myself very hungry. She gave me second helpings and then I lay down for a long sleep.

Next day Emmie visited me quite early. She said,

"I wanted to check you were quite alright. It's been all over the news about the demo at the back of the Minster... the Royal and the

runaway pig... they haven't yet worked out that it's Patrick White the singing and dancing pig."

"Oink... thank goodness," I replied. "Yes, I am alright now but yesterday was a horrible day. I understand less and less about humans."

Indeed, I was quite shaken up and I even began to wonder about the wisdom of being a talking pig. Over the next few weeks things began to get back to normal. I had visits from Letitia, Rebecca and Aaron and Charlie. I was pleased the media had not made any more of the story of the runaway pig. I watched a little television and managed to get some literature on screen to read.

For quite a while I felt rather gloomy. Emmie had me take care of some gilts so that she would have some piglets but even that did not cheer me up. Charlie brought me some beer. I did enjoy that to some extent. I had a chat with Rebecca about the confusing nature of the human world. I enjoyed my human comforts, and it was evident things could not be the same as when I arrived on the farm. I did not, however, wish to go out into the human world any more or be known for singing and dancing on social media.

As time passed, I came to a decision.

(ii) Was it all a dream?

I woke up on 1 April with the oddest feeling. I had the impression that I had the strangest dream that Percival the pig had learned to speak, and we had had all sorts of adventures, over the last year. There seemed to be a court case where he had met the judge. He had even somehow changed his name. I wondered if I had eaten something which had disagreed with me.

Piecrust the dog slept across my feet as usual. My alarm went off at quarter to seven. I began to stir. I went to the bathroom briefly and came back and sat down. I switched on the radio. The announcer said,

"Good morning on this bright and breezy April Fools' Day. First the weather and then the news headlines…"

The weather forecast was good. I turned off the radio before the news. I didn't want to hear a load of gloom. I had a very quick bath while Piecrust looked on. I dried off pulled on my clothes and went downstairs. Empress, Princess and Duchess, the cats, all lined up by their bowls awaiting their breakfast.

"Miaow," they said in a chorus.

I had a large mug of coffee and some toast and honey while Piecrust munched on some dog biscuits.

It was time to start seeing to the farm animals. Scuffy would be along shortly to help but feeding Percival was my duty. There seemed to be no April fools' jokes from Alain. He had just left a fine Chablis in the fridge with a little note stuck on it 'To enjoy together when I am home'.

I pulled on my boots and slung on an old jacket. I headed outside to the brick stables at the side of the house. The music from the radio was playing softly in the background.

"Morning. Oink. Emmie," came a voice I knew I recognised. I smiled. Somehow I was relieved to be having this conversation. Patrick continued, "I have made a decision. First, I don't want to leave the farm ever again. Oink… I certainly don't want to be an expert witness again or dance or sing for social media. However, I have decided to write my memoirs and YOU are going to help me."

Notes and Acknowledgements

First this is a work of fiction, and it does not pretend to give guidance or show any expertise on pig keeping. However, I must acknowledge being a regular reader of 'Practical Pigs' magazine. I can also recommend 'Raising Pigs' by Lee Faber published by Abbeydale Press. Further information on pig welfare can be found on www.britishpigs.org and of course with the RSPCA. 'The Country Smallholder' magazine published by Kelsey Media often has interesting information about pigs. Its predecessor 'Country Smallholding' published by Archant had a particularly apt article written by Mandy Rickaby called 'The pig paradox' in the November 2021 edition.

There is information on animal vocalisations on the website of the Zoological Society of London
https://zslpublications.onlinelibrary.wiley.com/doi/10.1111/j.1469-7998.2012.00920.x.

More scientific minds than mine would have to explain 'source filter theory' and the various abilities or otherwise of animals to speak.

As for the procedures surrounding civil trials in England and Wales, the current regime came into force in the Civil Procedure Rules 1998

https://www.legislation.gov.uk/uksi/1998/3132/contents/made.

They have been much amended.

See https://www.justice.gov.uk/courts/procedure-rules/civil.

For more information about courts in England and Wales see the website for HMCTS

https://www.gov.uk/government/organisations/hm-courts-and-tribunals-service.

For information about the rules governing solicitors see the Solicitors' Regulation Authority website

https://www.sra.org.uk/.

The Bar Council's website is

https://www.barcouncil.org.uk/.

Was there a St Rita? As I understand it, she was a nun who persevered through a lifetime of disappointments and became the Patron Saint of the Impossible.

Could there be a Patrick White out there? I am not qualified to say.

Printed in Great Britain
by Amazon